FLORENCE PARKER SIMISTER

Cover design by Elle Staples
Cover illustration by Rebecca Sorge
Originally published in 1959
© 2019 Jenny Phillips
goodandbeautiful.com
All rights reserved. No portion of this book may be reproduced in any form without permission from the publisher.

Table of Contents

Chapter One. 1

Chapter Two. 10

Chapter Three .18

Chapter Four 28

Chapter Five. 37

Chapter Six. 45

Chapter Seven .54

Chapter Eight. .63

Chapter Nine 74

EXPLANATORY NOTE

This is a novel based on the life of a real girl, Deborah Sampson, who served in the Revolutionary War as a soldier in the Fourth Massachusetts Regiment commanded by Colonel William Shepherd of Westfield. Her biography was written by Herman Mann and was called *Life of Deborah Sampson: The Female Soldier in the War of the Revolution*. It was printed by Nathaniel and Benjamin Heaton in Dedham, Massachusetts, in 1797.

In addition to basing my fictional heroine on a real person, I have based the military action on fact. The capture of General Prescott, the ambushing of the British on Prudence Island, the mutiny in the camp—these and all the other military events are part of the history of Rhode Island.

F. S.

Chapter One

"No," Anne Saunders repeated, and shook her head to emphasize the point. "No, Sam, I will not marry you."

She could feel his eyes searching her face for some sign of weakening. Then he dropped them to the hand bill he had brought her announcing the occupation of Newport to the British. He looked at the piece of paper as if that were the reason for her refusal. Finally, his eyes met hers again.

"I always thought," he said softly, "that you would someday be my wife."

"I never meant you to understand that," Anne protested.

"But, Anne, you walked with me, rode with me, talked with me. . ."

Anne broke in, "Oh, Sam, yes, I talked with you, I walked with you, I rode with you, and if I become your wife, we would do that all our lives. That would be safe and pleasant, I know."

"I would try to make your life secure," Sam said. Then he added quickly before she could speak, "Besides, you would have your own house, your own things, different from the way you live now."

"Yes," she said, "it is tempting, what you offer me. But there is more to life than that." She tapped the handbill on the table. "And more than this little town." Her voice became intense. "I want more, do you hear? I want more from life than that!"

"More?" Sam asked. He came forward to the table. His long, thin body was tense. His large hands rolled and rerolled the brim of his hat. His gentle, plain face was flushed. "What more is there in life than love and peace?" he asked.

"But there is no peace!" Anne flung his words back at him. "We are fighting a war! The Redcoats have just taken Newport. And love—well, that has to wait in time of war." She put a hand on Sam's arm. "Sam," she said pleadingly, "all my life I worked for others, did for others. I was only ten when I came here to the Brownes' to work. I don't blame my aunt for sending me out; she couldn't keep an orphan any longer. For eight years now I have worked for the Brownes and had to scheme to get a bit of learning for myself. Now they allow me to use the parlor as a school, but a dame school is of no importance in these times. There is a war being waged, a revolution, and I want to be a part of it! Teaching children isn't part of it." Softly she added, "You are a good man, Sam, but marrying you isn't part of it, either."

"What is then?" asked Sam.

Before Anne could answer, the sound of a fife and drum drifted to them from the far end of the common on which the house stood.

"Another band of soldiers leaving," said Anne. "That's a part of it, Sam! Oh, what I would give to be going. What I would give!"

As the fife and drum became louder, she went to the window. A small group of men marched down the road past the house. They carried old muskets and powder horns taken from over the mantles of their homes. They wore breeches and leather aprons and waistcoats and hunting shirts.

"Soldiers!" snorted Sam behind her. "They look no more like soldiers than . . ."

Anne whirled on him. "What does it matter what they wear?" she cried. "They are patriots!"

Sam interrupted. "I am a patriot, too," he said in a voice that was not quite angry but was gruff with emotion. "You forget, Anne, that I offered my services. I wanted to enlist, but they refused me because I make bayonets in my blacksmith shop.

They need bayonets just as they need the paper from Mr. Brownes' mill to wrap the cartridges. These are weapons of war!" He stopped abruptly. He looked as if he were sorry for his outburst.

"Very well," said Anne. "You are exempted from fighting because you make bayonets. Mr. Browne is exempted because he manufactures paper. But I am not exempted for keeping a dame school, and I wish I were going off to battle!"

Anne changed the tone of her voice. "What can women do?" she asked mournfully "What share can we take in the war except to work the farms and spin and do men's chores where needed?" Her voice was full of passion again. "Mrs. Brownes' only son, her only child, was killed at Lexington, and all she can do is sit and knit socks for the soldiers. Am I to be condemned to that, too? Oh, how I wish I were going off to battle!"

Sam seized her wrist. "I wish you were going to marry me, Anne," he said in the most desperate tone Anne had ever heard him use.

Stubbornly she shook her head.

"Will you remember, then," he asked, "that I will be here in my blacksmith shop if ever you want me? Will you remember that I love you? Will you remember that through all this war, through whatever it is you will do?"

"I will remember," Anne promised, and looked for a long time into his kind blue eyes.

Quickly then he leaned over and brushed his lips against the cap she wore on her hair, turned on his heel, and left the house.

Anne stood there alone in the room, thinking of Sam Prentice, blacksmith, the man she had gone to watch at his father's forge when she first came to this town of Brownes' Mill. She had been a child of ten then, Sam about fifteen. He had taught her so much. He had talked to her of books and book learning. He had suggested the idea of starting a school and had persuaded Mrs. Browne to let her do it. Sam would make a steady husband, thought Anne. He had offered her a place she could call home for the first time in her life, her own house, her own things. It was a safe and sure life, but it had nothing to do with the war for independence.

She heard running footsteps and turned again to the window. A boy, hardly more than thirteen or fourteen, carrying a musket whose weight seemed more than he could manage, ran down the road after the group that had just passed.

Going to Providence to enlist, thought Anne. The size of him! Why, I'm bigger than he is. If he can fight, why can't I? She gasped at the thought that struck her. Why couldn't I fight, if I were dressed in a man's clothes?

Her knees began to shake at the boldness of the idea. She sank into a chair and thought about it. There were all of young Robert Brownes' clothes upstairs in his room, all the things he left behind when he went off to war. They would fit her fairly well, no doubt, but would she look like a boy in them?

As soon as this question occurred to Anne, she climbed the stairs to find the clothes and try them on. She opened the door to Robert's room and entered quietly, closing it behind her. She took off her mobcap and her dress and apron. In a chest she found breeches, a shirt, and a waistcoat. In a cupboard there were shoes and a hat. She put on the breeches, the shirt, and the waistcoat, and rejoiced that her legs were long and thin and that the waistcoat was full enough so that it disguised her form. With one hand she pulled her hair back from her face and held it, while with the other she clapped the hat on her head.

She turned to see if there was a mirror, and as she did, she saw her reflection in the window. She stared. It was hard to believe, but she looked like a fairly tall, thin boy with dark hair and eyes. Quickly she picked up her own clothes and climbed the stairs to her small room under the eaves. There she stowed away what she had selected of Robert's clothes and put her own back on.

I will venture it sometime, she thought, perhaps this very evening at the tavern. If I can pass as a boy once, I can do it again. I can enlist!

The rest of that day was a misery to Anne. She was allowed by the Brownes to keep school in the morning for the neighbors' little children. In the afternoon she still had all kinds of duties to perform. She prepared supper. She cleaned the kitchen. She worked at the loom. The day, as usual, was full of activities, but the idea that had come to her buzzed in her head, no matter what chore she was doing.

After supper was over, she sat at the kitchen table and arranged lessons for the next day. She was impatient for the time when the Brownes would go to bed. Her heart beat fast with excitement, and the time seemed endless.

Then the sound she had been waiting for came at last. There were footsteps, and Mr. Browne stood at the kitchen door with Mrs. Browne.

He said the words he had repeated to her every evening for eight years. "Time to have your rest, Anne. God be with you this night."

Anne banked the fire, then picked up her candle and followed the couple up the stairs. For the first time she noticed that they seemed to sag with age, or with grief for their son. The two old people entered their room and closed the door, and she continued up to her room. Once there, she stripped off her own clothes and with shaking hands put on Robert Brownes', all but the shoes. She searched for a few pennies and found them at the bottom of a box. She needed some money, for she had decided she would go to the Greenbush Tavern at the other end of the common to test her disguise.

Anne walked up and down her room trying to get used to the feel of breeches, of her hair tied back with a ribbon. Then she sat for a long time waiting to make sure Mr. and Mrs. Browne were asleep.

At last, with her heart pounding, Anne blew out her candle and started down the stairs. She carried her shoes in her hand.

Slowly down the first flight she went, slowly down the second. Not a board creaked to give her away. Out to the kitchen she tiptoed. She lifted the bolt, opened the door, and closed it gently behind her. Weak with the strain of trying to be quiet, she sat on the back step and put on her shoes. The first part of her plan had gone well.

When she caught her breath, she walked around to the front of the house and stood looking at the town bathed in moonlight. White houses were set in a ring facing a grassy plot which the townspeople called a common. The road ran between the houses and the common. At one end of the town were the church and the mill, at the other the Greenbush Tavern and the blacksmith shop. Fanning out from this center were the farms of the neighborhood.

Brownes' Mill is a dear town, thought Anne, a peaceful town, but too quiet, too safe for me with all the important happenings that are going on out in the world.

A horse clattered down the road on one side of the common, and Anne stepped into the deep shadow of a tree until horse and rider had passed. Then she started down the road.

As she approached the Greenbush Tavern, her courage drained out of her. She sat down on a stone wall for a moment and looked at the lighted windows. Then from the barn behind the tavern she heard a shot of laughter, men's loud laughter.

They are playing skittles in the barn, thought Anne. Why do I not go out there instead of into the taproom?

At that thought, she got up from the wall, threw back her shoulders, and hastened toward the barn behind the tavern where the skittles alley was.

Her heart pounded with excitement, but no one looked at her as she slipped through the doorway. Several men stood around smoking their churchwarden pipes, the long white pipe that

Mr. Browne and Sam smoked, too. Candles burned in brackets hung from the beams and shed a dim light over the players and the watchers.

As she stood there, Anne's heart gradually slowed to a normal beating, for no one stared at her suspiciously. I must appear to be a lad, she thought, and smiled. She began to enjoy herself and watched, too, while some men set up the sticks of wood at one end of the alley. Two men picked up the balls, and each in turn rolled his at the sticks of wood which Anne knew were called skittles. She had often heard Sam and Robert Browne talk about this game.

The audience made no sound while the players made their shots, but after each play they removed the pipes from their mouths long enough to cheer or grunt or mutter.

The ball looked large. A foot across, I'll wager, thought Anne, and it is lopsided as I have often been told. How can they roll it then, she wondered.

She stood on tiptoe to peer at the next player. He took one step forward, rolled his ball, and knocked over all the skittles! The men murmured praise, and there were a few shouts.

The player straightened up and wiped his hands on his breeches. His face wore a satisfied smile. He looked at the men and, with what Anne thought was a sneer, he said, "If there is anyone who can equal that, I pledge you all a tot of rum."

The men stood silent. It seemed to Anne that perhaps they had heard these words before. Then, suddenly, an old man in the corner stepped forward. His eyes darted from one man to another and fastened on Anne. "You!" he called out, pointing at her with his pipe. "You are new here. Come and try your luck."

Anne shrank back, afraid. Everyone turned to stare, and she wished that the floor would open up and swallow her.

The old man spoke again. "Come, try your luck," he said. "Everyone else here has tried. Allen has pledged us rum. Step forward, lad! Give him a ball, Allen," he commanded the man who had just knocked over all the skittles.

Allen picked up a ball and held it toward Anne, but she was so frightened that she could not move to take it. At that moment she felt herself pushed from behind, a strong push that sent her stumbling toward the outstretched hand.

She took the ball, almost dropped it in her nervousness, and walked slowly to the end of the alley. She felt every eye on her, and the ball seemed tremendous in her hand. Her mind churned with the possible results of failure or success, but one thought was uppermost: they take me for a lad! This seemed to give her strength and courage.

She drew back her arm and rolled the ball down the alley. She held her breath, hardly daring to look as it reached the skittles. All but one fell over . . . and then that, too, rocked and fell! Anne let out her breath and stood and stared. There were loud cheers, and she felt her knees start to tremble.

"What's wrong with you, lad?" asked the old man in his gruff voice. "You astonished?"

Anne shook her head as if to settle her brains back into working order. She must not let on that this was her first game of skittles or that she was amazed at her luck with the ball. "Astonished?" she repeated. "No." Then, in a bragging tone of voice, she added, "I knew I could do it."

The old man laughed and came up to her. "Into the taproom," he said. "We have been pledged a tot of rum, have we not?" he asked Allen.

Allen looked surly, but he muttered, "I will keep my pledge."

The old man threw an arm around Anne's shoulders. She shrank away from him. "Thank you," she said, "but I must be on my way. It is late."

"Stranger around here, aren't you?" asked Allen.

"No," Anne answered, anxious now to leave. "I live yonder." She pointed with her thumb over her shoulder.

"What did you say your name was, lad?" asked the man.

"Anne . . ." she replied automatically, while her mind leaped wildly about. ". . . drew," she added quickly. "Andrew Saunders," she said almost inaudibly. She had not been prepared with a new name.

He misunderstood. "Sands?" he repeated. "Never knew anyone by that name. Long way to go?"

"Long enough," Anne replied. "A good night to you all." She thrust her hands into the pockets of her waistcoat and swaggered out the door ahead of them.

As she reached the road there was a burst of laughter from the men just entering the taproom of the tavern. She felt color mount to her cheeks. Had they said something about her? Then she assured herself that if they had, it was not about her, but about the boy she had become. She had posed as a lad and been taken for one! She laughed quietly in the dark and walked swiftly home.

She felt jubilant, for this meant she could do what she yearned to do: enlist. And thanks to the farmers, she had a new name to go with her new clothes.

In this way, on a moonlit night in December of the year 1776, Andrew Sands was born.

Chapter Two

A few nights later Anne again sat in her room dressed in waistcoat, shirt, and breeches, waiting for the house to settle into its nightly quiet. This time, as Andrew Sands, she planned to walk down the Post Road to the Dragon, the inn at the crossroads where the wagoners, the post riders, and the stage stopped, to find out about enlisting.

Anxiously she sat in the dark watching until the path of moonlight on the wall of her room moved across to her bed. When that much time passed, she considered it safe to leave.

She turned at the door. A second she stood there looking at the room in the moonlight before she started down the stairs carrying her shoes in her hand. Quickly this time she went down the two flights to the kitchen and out the door. She stopped to put on her shoes, then started off in the direction of the church.

It was December and, although there was no snow, it was too cold to be outdoors wearing only a waistcoat over a shirt and breeches, but Robert Browne had not left a coat at home. Anne shivered and thrust her hands deep into her pockets. She strode along briskly, walking as she thought a boy would walk.

The bare branches of the trees rubbed together dryly in the wind. Anne's footsteps rang out loudly in the cold, clear air. She jingled the coins in her pocket, the same coins she had carried a few nights before, and quickened her pace.

Something moved in the bushes at the side of the road. Anne stopped, and there was a sensation of fear at the pit of her stomach. It occurred to her that if she met an animal, she was completely unarmed, but whatever was in the underbrush did not come out, and the fright passed.

Anne went on and soon reached a fork in the road. This fork, she knew, was not much below the crossroads where the Dragon was located. She felt just as excited as the first time, just as daring, and, as she caught her first glimpse of the lights of the inn, she felt just as frightened, too. She was tempted to turn back, but she squared her shoulders and walked on. There were several horses tied to the palings of the fence outside the inn, and Anne could hear the murmur of a great many voices.

She opened the door and saw that the taproom was crowded, so crowded that no one paid any attention to her. She was grateful for that. She ordered a pot of hot mulled ale, although she had no idea of drinking it, and while she waited for it, she looked around carefully to see if anyone was there who might know her. She recognized no one.

Carrying the pot of ale in two hands to warm them, she strolled around the room slowly, aimlessly. She watched some men at a table playing backgammon and some others at a nearby table playing draughts. Anne understood neither game well, so she drifted on. Before the fire, on the other side of the room, there lay or sat or squatted several young men.

They will know about enlisting, thought Anne. She approached them.

"Good evening," she said. She was so frightened that her voice quivered.

"Welcome," one of the men replied. He smiled and waved a tankard at her.

He was dark and thin and handsome, and Anne judged that he would be tall when he stood up.

"Aiming to enlist?" he asked.

Anne was delighted with the question. He takes me for a boy, she thought. "Yes," she answered, "how did you know?"

"Well," he explained, "the call went out for volunteers. This is the Post Road to Providence. What would you be doing here otherwise? Don't spend much time in taverns generally, do you?" His smile deepened as if to take away any hurt in his words. "We are on our way to Providence, too," he added. "Join us."

A short, thick fellow with red hair who sat looking at the fire turned around slowly and stared at Anne. It was an insulting look; it took her in from top to toe. Anne felt a blush rising in her cheeks, and she began to tremble. Finally he turned to the dark, thin one and said, "Why don't you ask children, too?"

The thin, dark man said, "Never heard that you owned the war, Tom."

"I don't," snarled Tom. "You can have the blasted revolution. I'll go home to my pigs." He struggled to get to his feet.

Another man in the group reached out as if to stop him from doing anything foolish. He must have caught him off balance, for Tom fell back and knocked over his tankard with a clatter.

Tom swore and started up as if to come to blows with everyone. Anne turned quickly and walked away. She could hear Tom shouting and all his friends trying to quiet him. Once she heard him say, "It's Joel's fault. Why does he talk to everyone, even children?"

Joel, thought Anne. That must be the name of the thin, dark one. Joel. And by children he means me.

She realized then for the first time that in boy's clothes she must look younger than her real age of eighteen. She would claim sixteen if anyone asked her.

She stood and watched the men in the room, her mind in a tumult. If these young men were really going to Providence to enlist, she would like to go with them. It would be a much easier thing to do with all of them than by herself, and she did want to have a part in the war for independence. And yet . . .

She had a moment of doubt. Was being a soldier what she really wanted to do?

At that instant all the voices in the room seemed to die away,

Chapter Two

all but one. That voice reached her clearly. At a crowded table near the window she could see the man who was speaking. He wore a powdered wig and lace at his cuffs. He pounded the table as he said, "Not for pay and rations, but to secure liberty and our independence!"

Yes, thought Anne, becoming determined again. To secure liberty and our independence. That is why I am here in the midst of these men. I, too, want to help.

She jumped and almost spilled her ale when a voice said in her ear, "You haven't drunk any of that."

She looked up at Joel, for it was he.

He smiled in a teasing way. "Come back now if you like," he said. "Tom has gone home to his pigs."

Anne turned toward him. "Am I to blame?"

"No," he answered. "He was trying to find an excuse to go home. He wasn't fond of coming in the first place. If there is a choice between pigs and seeing the world, Tom chooses pigs."

They walked back to the fire and Joel's friends. He introduced them. "Israel is over there—" he pointed to a small man. "And Nick." He must be the oldest, thought Anne. "And Will, Nick's brother." Will was the image of Nick, only younger. "And my name is Joel."

Anne was prepared. She said, "And mine is Andrew Sands. Andy."

Joel lifted his tankard and drank. "You going to Providence?"

Anne nodded and pretended to take a sip of ale.

"What do you do when you're not soldiering?"

"I teach school," she said.

"A school teacher!" shouted Nick, and slapped his breeches in glee. "I wager I'm going to get an education in this war. What can a boy like you teach me?" He laughed uproariously.

"What do you do?" Anne asked Joel as soon as the laughter subsided.

Joel pointed to his friends one by one. "Tinker," he explained.

"Ropemaker. Ropemaker like his brother." He pointed to himself. "Farmer. Sit down, Andy." He indicated the floor.

Anne sat awkwardly, so awkwardly that she spilled the ale all over her breeches. She brushed the wet places with her hand and moved closer to the fire. She was nervous, and perspiration made her hands moist. She was afraid that somehow she would give herself away, that these men would discover her disguise. She took off her hat, leaned her head against the stone of the fireplace, and closed her eyes.

"Walked far today, Andy?" asked Joel.

Her eyes flew open. "Yes," she answered. "Far enough." She asked. "Are you going on tonight?"

"Not I," answered Joel. "I'm sleeping in the Dragon. We have permission to stay right here on this floor where its warm."

Israel spoke for the first time. "We're going to start out again at cockcrow. We're going to enlist in the troops guarding Rhode Island. Fifteen months' service. Six pounds bounty." He looked surprised at how much he had said and became silent again.

Troops guarding Rhode Island, thought Anne. Suddenly this seemed important: to stay in Rhode Island.

Nick laughed again. "Thinkin' it over now?" he asked.

Will said, "You can still go home, Andy. General Washington doesn't know you're comin'."

Anne blushed.

"Leave the boy alone," Joel said roughly. "How old are you?" he asked Anne.

"Sixteen," Anne answered, and stammered over the age in spite of herself.

Will and Nick smiled at each other. Nick winked. "Sixteen?" he drawled, implying that fourteen would have been nearer the truth.

"That's good enough," Joel said quickly. "Sixteen to sixty is what they're taking."

"Will they take me, do you think?" Anne asked him.

"Don't know why not. You're a boy," said Joel.

Anne quickly raised her tankard to hide her face.

"You're not crippled," Joel continued. "Can you shoot?"

"Yes," said Anne, happy to be giving a truthful answer for once.

"They'll take you," Nick promised. "We'll make 'em." He yawned loudly. "When do we sleep?" he asked.

"Now," answered Will, and lay down on the floor and put his hat over his face.

Anne looked around. The crowd had thinned. Some candles on sconces on the walls had been snuffed out. The room was full of shadows. She argued in her mind about staying or not staying with these men. Joel seemed to think she was a young boy who needed help. That would be a good thing, to have a friend like Joel. If she really wanted to enlist, this would be a fine way to do it. She was frightened, but it would be worse if she were alone. She decided she would throw in her lot with these men.

"If you do not mind," she said timidly, "I will go to Providence with you."

"Come along," said Joel. "Let us sleep now. The Dragon will be empty in no time."

Joel was right; almost nobody was left at the tables. Anne felt panic rise in her. She wanted to get up and go, too. She forced herself to remain where she was. With all the willpower at her command, she forced down the panic and stayed on the floor.

She saw the innkeeper pick up the glasses and tankards, lock up the place where the casks of ale and rum were kept, bolt the door, and go upstairs, carrying the last candle. She almost ran after him. She almost cried out, but she didn't.

Now the room was in darkness except for some embers glowing in the fireplace. Anne didn't dare move. She was hot, uncomfortable, and terrified. Between the bangings and creakings of the house, the snores of her companions, and the cracklings in the fireplace, she stayed awake. She lay the whole night alternating between terror at what she had done and determination to fight for Rhode Island and the rest of the colonies. The call had gone out for volunteers. They needed everyone they could get to defend the shores of the mainland now that the British held Newport down the bay.

In the morning her desire to fight for the cause of liberty was still strong. With the coming of daybreak, she came to two decisions. She decided to enlist, and she decided to let Sam know that she had gone away.

When it was light, she got up off the floor. None of the men stirred. She left them, and in a room across the hall from the taproom she found ink and a pen and a scrap of paper. She wrote: "Dear Sam, I am going away for a time. Please tell the Brownes. A. S."

She slipped the note into her pocket to be posted in Providence and went back to the taproom. She roused Joel and the rest and slowly they straggled out of the Dragon.

Outside they looked mussed and red-eyed, and each man in turn rubbed chin and cheeks which were dark with beard stubble. Furtively Anne touched her own smooth chin.

Joel saw her and laughed. "No beard, Andy?" he asked.

Anne felt alarmed. She had succeeded in drawing attention to herself. She didn't answer.

"No matter," said Joel, and yawned. "A beard doesn't make a man."

"It makes a man itchy," said Israel.

They all laughed, and then Joel began to whistle, softly, tunelessly. They all fell in step to it and started up the road toward the army headquarters in Providence.

The town, when they reached it, looked like an armed camp, and a wave of patriotism engulfed Anne at the sight of soldiers in uniform and cannon bristling in a fort near the harbor. A few minutes later, at headquarters, trembling, she put her name on a paper that began:

Chapter Two

"I, the subscriber, do hereby solemnly engage and enlist myself as a soldier in the pay of the State of Rhode Island and Providence Plantations, for the preservation of the liberties of America, and the defence of the United States in general, and of this state in particular . . ."

Later in the day Anne stood on a parade ground with the other men who had enlisted. One by one they answered their names, which were called out by an officer. In this way they were all put on a muster roll. Each of them was given four pieces of paper money, the bounty money promised them for enlisting. Anne looked at hers. On each piece were the words "THIRTY SHILLINGS."

Quickly she calculated. One hundred and twenty shillings altogether. Twenty shillings made a pound. Six pounds! That is more money than I have ever had before in my life, she thought. She tucked it deep down in the pocket of her waistcoat where it would be safe. I have six pounds, she thought, and I am on the muster roll of the army!

Soon she and her new friends set off on foot for a place on the shore of Narragansett Bay called Warwick Neck, which was to be guarded against raids by the British.

Chapter Three

There were no tents or huts at Warwick Neck. The enlisted men were quartered in the barn loft, the officers in a farmhouse.

It was dusk when Anne and her friends reached the place, but they could see that the men in the camp had already built a fort on a height overlooking the bay.

The banks from the breastworks down to the water's edge look easy for the enemy to scale, thought Anne, if they come this way.

Across a short stretch of water, they could see the islands of Patience and Prudence, and Anne knew that east of Prudence lay the island of Newport. The bay was dotted with islands, like stepping stones to the mainland.

Joel put her thoughts into words. "If the British were to land here," he said, "and were not stopped, they could be in Providence in less than four hours."

"They will not get by if they come," Nick said, and Anne was amazed at the determination in his voice.

"The whole bay bristles with posts like this," Will added. "Pray Heaven, we'll bottle 'em up in Newport!"

"Amen," whispered Anne fervently.

For a moment they stood silent, overcome by their wish for freedom and by love for this land that bordered the sea. Then, as one man, they turned and went to the farmhouse headquarters to report.

After mess it became bitter cold, and the men, except for those on guard duty, crowded into the barn. Anne and her friends climbed to the loft, but most of the company were there before them, lolling and talking. No candles had been issued, and there were no blankets. Anne was grateful for the dark, for she did not have the strength to meet the stares of the other men in the company.

The dark was welcome, but the cold was not. It was a penetrating cold. Anne pulled her knees up to her chin and hugged them and tried to sleep. She realized that she was deathly tired. For a moment there flashed across her mind's eye the vision of her room at the Brownes', with the soft, clean bed and the warm quilts.

She must have stirred or sighed, for Joel's voice near her asked, "Is something the matter?"

"No," answered Anne. "It is just that I am so tired."

"So are we all, Andy. We have come a long way today."

A long way, indeed, thought Anne. She felt a hand clap her lightly on the shoulder in an encouraging, brotherly fashion. It was Joel's hand. How good of him, she thought. He believes I am a homesick lad. All day he has been as kind to me as a brother. She breathed deeply, trying to ease the feeling of tiredness.

The men around her grumbled because there were no candles, no soap. They complained about the rations, that the gill of rum promised to them had not been issued. Then, suddenly, sweetly from the far corner of the loft came the sound of a flute. Sam played a flute, and for a moment Anne was transported back in memory to the millpond on a summer's evening, with Sam sitting on a stump playing the songs he loved.

In the loft a voice joined the flute, singing, "All people that on earth do dwell." The men fell silent, listening, but as soon as the hymn ended, the grumbling began all over again. The men's voices seemed to Anne to swell and ebb as she fell into a kind of half sleep. She was roused by one clear thought: I am not afraid anymore of Joel and his friends. They take me for a lad. She smiled. Then she slept.

The next minute, or so it seemed to Anne, cutting through the relaxed dark came the sound of the drums beating reveille, calling them out. Anne could not believe it was morning. She struggled to her feet, still groggy with weariness.

When assembly was drummed, the men walked to the parade ground, a cleared flat piece of land beyond the barn. Faint light in the eastern sky showed that it was really daybreak.

On her first day as a soldier, Anne had a fluttering feeling of excitement. She looked straight ahead and tried to make herself as inconspicuous as possible. She needn't have worried; no one noticed her.

The roll was called and coats and blankets were dealt out to those who had none. Anne was grateful for the warmth of a coat. Her waistcoat had not been enough for December weather. Now she felt almost like a soldier.

Her first orders, though, were not warlike. She and several men were sent to a barn about a mile down the road to load the hay there into wagons.

Israel was one of the file of men, the only one of her friends.

They walked in silence. Anne felt as if she were walking in her sleep. Neither the breakfast of bread and coffee nor the roll call had helped to awaken her much.

Israel finally spoke. "Everything's got to be moved inland—away from the British, is that it?"

"I reckon so," said a man behind Anne. "Lobsterbacks won't stop at anything to get forage for their animals. Been up as far as Prudence once. Why not Warwick Neck? Burnin' and plunderin' as they go. We're to move everything one and a half miles inland, I understand—all hay, grain, and stock."

"That is hard for the owners, isn't it?" asked Anne.

"Better than havin' it feed the British," the man answered vehemently and so definitely that there was nothing to be added.

They walked the rest of the way in silence until they came in sight of the barn. It was a monstrous structure, but they did not have long to look at it. The officer in charge urged them to walk faster, to find pitchforks, to set up.

The wagons were put in position to receive the hay. Some men went to the loft to drop the hay, some stood on the wagons. Anne was one of those on the wagons, building the load. She had done this many times before and knew how to do it properly, for Mr. Browne had taught her how to load and unload hay and how to avoid putting her feet on the hay she was trying to lift.

In spite of the cold, it was hot, thirsty work. The new coat which had felt so good on the parade ground seemed heavy now. Anne put it to one side and looked enviously at the canteens of water which some of the men carried. No one offered her a drink, and she refused to ask for one.

I can do without it, she thought. Secretly she felt proud of herself for knowing how to load hay and for being able to work as hard as a man.

When the loading was finished, the wagons clattered off. The men marched back to camp through a dull landscape where no other living thing moved. The sun did not shine, and the wind was rising. It felt like snow.

Back at Warwick Neck there was much excitement. The quartermaster had arrived with chests of arms and cartridges and a twelve-pound cannon to add to the two eighteen-pounders already in the fort. Some men had been put to work building a field carriage for the cannon, and the firearms were being dealt out.

Anne stood in line to receive hers. The lieutenant was precise in making sure that the bullets fitted the bore of the musket. Then she was given a cartridge box, holding seventeen rounds, two flints, and a musket. The lieutenant chose seventeen more cartridges and wrapped them in paper.

"Name?" he asked.

"Sands," said Anne. "Andrew Sands."

He wrote her name on the paper and put the package to one side. "In case of an alarm," he said, tapping the paper-wrapped cartridges, "these will be delivered to you."

"Yes, sir," Anne said.

He wrote something on a slip of paper and turned it toward her. "Sign this showing you have received your musket and seventeen rounds," he ordered.

For the second time Anne wrote "Andrew Sands," and then picked up her musket and cartridge box. Now, she thought, I am a soldier. I have a coat, a musket, and a cartridge box. The musket was heavy, but Anne had used Sam's many times to shoot rabbits and groundhogs, and she was used to it.

She turned and started for the barn, but the drum began to beat assembly, so she ran to the parade ground instead, gasping for breath because of the weight of the musket.

Joel stood at her side. "Express rider came," he said, as if that explained their presence on the parade ground. "I'm on fatigue duty," he offered. "Sawing wood."

"I was pitching hay," Anne told him, "so the British won't get it."

They formed ranks and stood waiting until the officer of the day appeared. Joel squinted up at the sky. "If the sun were shining, I'd say it would be about six hours high. Hard to tell without the sun."

Somewhere across the water a cannon went off.

"What is that?" asked Anne.

"Alarm gun," Joel explained.

A man on the other side of Anne said, "They go off all the time. Don't concern us."

"Why did they shoot it off?"

"Must have thought they seen a Redcoat. Some people sees 'em in trees and behind bushes, and no wonder, there's nigh unto ten thousand down the bay."

"'Ten thousand!" Anne looked around at the handful of men. Of course she knew there were many other forts like this one all round the bay, but ten thousand British!

Chapter Three

The officer of the day, Captain Potter, appeared and bellowed at them, "I need two men for a particular job. Volunteers step forward three paces."

Out of the corner of her eye, Anne noticed that Joel tripped, then recovered his balance as the entire company moved forward three paces. Anne felt a thrill of pride because they all responded to the request for volunteers.

The officer pointed. "You and you," he said.

He pointed to Anne and Joel. They stepped forward. "Follow me," he ordered. He shouted at the men, "Dismissed."

Anne and Joel followed him back to the farmhouse. He took off his coat and hat and sat down at a table on which were pen, ink, and paper.

"At ease," he said.

Joel and Anne relaxed.

"There is a barn," he began, "where the state has stored its sugar. It was broken into last night and a fair amount of sugar stolen. We are to post guard there. You will be prepared to stay from midnight until dawn. You will not be visited by the captain of the guard; it is too far afield. You will apprehend anyone who approaches the building." He had been writing as he spoke. He now picked up the rudely drawn map. "I have marked the barn," he said, "and the road. Do you understand the map?"

Joel studied it for a second. "Yes, sir," he said.

"The countersign for tonight is 'Stand together.' Report to me when you come off duty."

Together Anne and Joel said, "Yes, sir."

"Dismissed," said Captain Potter.

Anne and Joel left the house and trudged back to quarters. They set to work to clean their muskets. They studied the map. The rest of the day passed quietly, and about eleven o'clock they started out. They were challenged by the sentry and gave the countersign. They were allowed to pass.

There was no moon; the stars were not visible. The sky had a heavy look of a sky full of snow. It was very cold. Beneath their feet the ground felt like stone. Anne dropped back a pace and let Joel lead. At the turn in the road, where a tavern stood, he struck off through a thicket.

She started to speak, but Joel said, "Better not talk," so she subsided into silence.

They went on for a long time, and Anne thought they must surely be lost, but suddenly they were out in the open again and on a cart path. They scaled a stone wall and struck across a meadow. Anne could now make out a mass looming up ahead. The barn, she thought.

A voice challenged them. "Who goes there?" The tone was so intense, and Anne was so startled by it, that she almost dropped her musket.

"Friends," Joel answered.

"Advance and be recognized. Give the countersign."

She and Joel gave it: "Stand together."

They came up to the guards they were relieving.

"Any thieves tonight?" asked Joel.

"None," the guard answered. "You know that the barn is full of hogsheads of sugar? The state's?"

"We know," said Joel.

"Guard it well," he warned. He picked up his knapsack and canteen, shouldered his musket. The second man did the same, and off they marched into the cold night. Anne and Joel were left to guard the sugar storehouse.

They walked around the barn and looked at the doors.

"I'll walk one side, you the other," suggested Joel.

Anne agreed, and they began to walk their posts. They spoke briefly as they met and stamped their feet and spanked their arms around themselves to keep warm. Joel whistled softly, tunelessly. Anne thought of Brownes' Mill and the excitement she had craved. She thought of the unbelievable fact that she was guarding the state's sugar supply in the countryside in the middle of a cold December night, and that the only person within the sound of her voice was a man, a stranger to her only a day ago.

But he doesn't seem strange, thought Anne. I feel as if I have always known Joel, as if he has always been my friend.

After several hours Anne began to hear voices where there were no voices, and footsteps approaching where there were no footsteps.

Three times she called out, "Who goes there?" only to be answered by the sharp crack of a tree in the cold. Every time she called out, Joel came running, and finally he said, "Andy, you are hearing things. You must be tired. Sleep a bit."

Anne said, "I dare not."

Joel insisted, "No one will know."

"Why are you so good to me?" Anne asked. She had wondered about this since she had met Joel. He had shared biscuits with her; he had bought her food at a tavern.

Joel answered in a voice so low that Anne had to strain to hear. "I had a young brother like you," he explained. "I was fond of him. He died last year. Smallpox."

"Oh," said Anne. She could think of nothing else to say. "Oh." She reached out a hand as if to touch him, but drew it back again, thinking perhaps men don't do that.

"Now you know," said Joel. Then, in his normal, gay tone of voice he added, "Take a nap, Andy."

Without further persuasion she agreed. "But wake me if you need me," she said.

Joel promised. She sat down in front of the small barn door, leaned back, and slept instantly.

How much later it was when she woke, she didn't know. The first thing she saw was flames. Joel was bending over a fire, which she now noticed was sheltered on three sides by large stones. His face in the firelight looked more handsome than ever. His expression was intent.

Anne's heart suddenly leaped as the flames leaped. A truth had become clear to her: she loved Joel. With this revelation came another. She loved him, but she could never tell him, for he thought she was a boy. He must never know, and she would have to act two parts now—the part of being a boy, and the part of a young brother instead of a sweetheart.

She blinked back tears that had sprung to her eyes. And then she wondered whether Joel should have built a fire. It could probably be seen over the whole countryside. She sat up abruptly.

"Oh," said Joel, "you're awake. I have a rabbit cooked. Hungry?"

"Yes," said Anne, and got to her feet. "Should you have built a fire?" she asked.

"Why not?" Joel answered. "Scare off the enemy! I'll put it out before the relief comes. Our time is almost up. It must be near daybreak."

"It was good of you to let me sleep." Anne took a deep breath and plunged into the acting of her new role. She said, "When I'm a full-grown man, I would like to be like you."

Joel gave her a quick look, and an odd expression crossed his face. He looked down at the fire, then offered her a piece of meat on the tip of his bayonet. "Extra rations," he said in a light tone of voice, and they began to eat. It was the gayest meal Anne had ever known. Joel knew many stories, and he told them with grace. He talked a great deal.

Not like Sam, thought Anne, who can sit for half an hour and never say a word. Anne was sad and happy at the same time . . . and content.

When they came off duty, they reported to Captain Potter. He dismissed Joel and said, "Sands, I would like a few words with you."

"Yes, sir," said Anne, quaking.

"I understand you are a schoolteacher. Is that true?" Captain Potter asked.

"Yes, sir," said Anne, wondering what would come next.

"I need some help in my office. I also need a waiter. Can you cook?"

"Y-yes, sir," Anne said again.

"I would like you to come to headquarters then. You will be required to cook and wait on tables and help to copy orders and dispatches."

Anne was disturbed. It would be easier for her to carry out her disguise at the farmhouse headquarters, but she had enlisted to fight, not to cook.

Captain Potter evidently saw the doubt in her face. "Does it not suit you?" he asked.

"It suits me," she answered, "but I wish to fight."

"Oh," said the captain, "we all have our posts in case of an alarm. You will have yours, too. You need not have concern about that."

"Then if I am given a chance to fight, sir, I will come."

"Good. Report this evening," he said. "Dismissed."

And so the rabbit supper was the first and would be the last meal she and Joel would eat alone together, for that evening, Anne moved to headquarters where she cooked and waited on tables and helped Captain Potter copy orders and dispatches.

Chapter Four

At headquarters in the farmhouse Anne slept on a sack in the warm kitchen so as to be ready to serve food and drink whenever an express rider or a visiting captain or colonel arrived. She was a waiter not only to Captain Potter but to his staff, Lieutenant Smith and Lieutenant Arnold, as well. Her day was a round of cooking, waiting on tables, and washing dishes. Many times she felt rebellious because she was doing what she had been doing at the Brownes' for so many years. But dreary monotony was the lot of everyone in the camp during the severe part of the winter when the snow fell without end and the drifts stood everywhere.

Some of the men spent their off-duty time at the tavern down the road; some had left camp, Israel, Nick, and Will among them. They had gone home to their families and farms. Joel stayed on. He told Anne that the monotony suited him.

The only excitement during the whole winter was the arrival of the express rider. Through him two wonderful pieces of news were relayed to the camp. In December they were told about the victorious battle of Trenton in New Jersey, and in January they heard about the success at Princeton. When the news was read to them on the parade ground, the men gave thirteen huzzahs for the thirteen states. They shouted so loud that Anne thought the British probably heard their voices down the bay in Newport.

As the days and weeks passed, Anne began to feel secure in her disguise. It was much easier now that she lived at headquarters, and she hardly ever worried any more about being found out. She felt she really was Andrew Sands.

Chapter Four

Once during the winter, though, she dreamed about Sam Prentice and awoke the next morning shaken because in the dream he had called, "Anne! Anne!" and it seemed to her that the name still reverberated in the kitchen. For a long time she had thought of writing to him. Now she did.

"I am well," she wrote, "and hope you are, too. Do not be concerned about my welfare. I would like the Brownes to know that I am well. A. S." She gave the note to the next express writer to be posted in Providence.

For some reason that seemed to free her of the image of Sam that had haunted her, but to rid herself of the thought of Joel seemed impossible. It was with her constantly, the thought of him and the memory of his face and the kind things he had said and done. Over and over she recounted them in her mind as some people count the coins in their purse.

When a day or two went by without seeing him except on the parade ground, she felt a yearning just to look at him. Then she would make some excuse to walk to the barn and talk to him. Sometimes Joel came to the farmhouse. He would stand on the far side of the sentry and whistle for her, and she would go and talk to him.

One day Anne was laying a fire in the dining room when she thought she heard the sound of a door opening and closing. She looked in the kitchen and the hall but saw no one. She finished laying the fire and went to the kitchen to fetch an ember in the fire scoop. On her way back to the dining room, she heard a sound again. This time she looked into the parlor which was now Captain Potter's office. A soldier, short, thick, and powerful, stood at Captain Potter's desk, throwing papers to the floor.

Anne called out, "What do you want?"

He whirled around.

"How did you get by the sentry?" Anne asked.

He smiled craftily, reached into his pocket, and held up a bludgeon.

Anne stepped back. "What do you want?" she asked again.

"I want my pay, that's what I want. I didn't get my pay. I need my pay. There's money here somewhere."

"There is no money here," Anne explained to him. "The paymaster will have it. You can't get it this way."

"Oh, can't I?" he asked. He walked across to her and stood, beating the palm of one hand with the thick end of the bludgeon.

Quickly Anne raised the fire scoop and, with all her strength, swung it sideways and hit him on the head over his ear.

He blinked once, then put back his head and laughed. "A young boy like you," he said, "tryin' to hit me?" He lunged at her.

Anne slipped by him and ran toward the kitchen. He overtook her just inside the door. He put out one huge hand and gathered up the front of her shirt and waistcoat in a bunch, lifting her off the floor and tightening the clothes around her throat so that she thought she would choke.

"I could crush your skull with one blow," he said. "You puny little boy. Not even a beard." He rubbed a thick, rough finger over her cheek and chin. He put his face right up to hers and said, "You ain't even got a beard. Are you even a boy?" His eyes looked at her malevolently.

Anne tried to speak, but no words came. Terror had made her dumb. Then, was she dreaming? She seemed to hear Joel's whistle. No, she wasn't dreaming. The man heard it, too, and his eyes shifted from right to left. The whistling stopped. They waited. Time seemed suspended. And then there were footsteps, and Joel stood in the doorway.

The man dropped Anne like a sack of meal and went after Joel, his bludgeon in his hand. Joel turned and ran off. Desperately, frantic with fear, Anne tried to call him back. She succeeded only in making a noise in her throat.

The man stood uncertainly for a moment, then started for the door, stopped, whirled around, and came toward Anne again. Anne tried to get up, but her legs wouldn't support her. At that moment, there was the pounding of boots in the hall, and the sentry entered the kitchen with Joel behind him. It took no time for them to subdue the man, and then, shakily, Anne got to her feet. She felt bewildered, sick.

"Andy?" asked Joel.

She nodded her head to show she was all right.

That was all the time they had, for at that moment Captain Potter arrived.

"What is taking place here?" he demanded. "Sands, are you turning my headquarters into a barracks?"

The sentry spoke. "This man crept up on me, sir. I was at my post. He hit me on the head with something."

"With this," said Joel, and picked up the bludgeon from the floor.

Anne rubbed her throat where her shirt had chafed it. She spoke quietly, "I was laying the fire in the dining room, sir, and heard a noise in your office. He"—she pointed at the man—"was going through the papers on your desk."

"Is this true?" Captain Potter asked the man.

He looked at the captain defiantly. "I didn't get my pay," he said. "I want my pay. I aim to get it. I need it."

"Pay!" the captain bellowed. "You came to steal pay? You assaulted the sentry? You assaulted my waiter? This will go hard with you. Your name?"

The man muttered, "Lawton."

"And who are you?" demanded the captain, suddenly whirling around on Joel.

"A friend of Andy, of Sands. The company was dismissed for the day. I walked over, and when I saw no sentry, I suspected there might be trouble."

"Is he a friend of yours?" the captain asked Anne.

"Yes, sir," she answered.

"Take him away," the captain ordered to the sentry, pointing at Lawton. "We shall deal with him. Sands, bring me a gill of rum."

"Yes, sir," said Anne.

"You," the captain said to Joel, "what is your name? In case we need you for evidence at the court-martial?"

"Sherman, sir," said Joel. "Joel Sherman."

"Dismissed, Sherman," said Captain Potter. With that he turned on his heel and went to his office.

Joel started to go but whispered to Andy, "I went to fetch the sentry because I didn't think I could subdue him alone. Are you hurt?"

"No," she said. Her hands shook as she filled a pewter gill measure with rum, then poured it into a glass.

She took the rum in to Captain Potter. He didn't look up from his writing, so she put it down on the desk and left.

On the way out she picked up her fire scoop. When she returned to the kitchen, Joel had gone. She went about her routine duties, but she was unnerved, shaken. A second longer, she felt, and she would have given away her secret, or he would have found out.

She was still in a nervous state when she returned to the farmhouse after giving evidence at the court-martial, which was held immediately. Lawton had been sentenced to thirty lashes, and all through the trial Anne had been the center of attention. Acutely conscious of her disguise and more apprehensive of discovery than at any time since her first visit to a tavern, she had left as soon as she could. Now she collapsed on her sack.

She fell into a restless sleep filled with dreams of Lawton, fire scoops, and Joel. She was roused from this sleep by the sound of marching feet and sat up with her heart racing. Had she slept through an alarm?

She stood up in the dark kitchen and, as she did so, heard the sound of footsteps. When she went into the hall, Captain Potter and the lieutenants were coming down the stairs carrying candles. They had evidently dressed hurriedly, for they wore only shirts and breeches.

"Sands," Captain Potter ordered, "fetch more candles. It sounds like trouble."

Anne rushed to the kitchen for more candles. The marching footsteps came nearer. Now, as Anne came back to the hall, she could hear loud talking, too.

Captain Potter put his candle on the table and threw open the door. There, approaching the sentry, was a group of men, how many it was impossible to say. Anne could see moonlight reflected from bayonets.

"Sentry!" thundered the captain, "Let one man pass."

"Yes, sir," came the reply.

In a moment a man came up the path from the gate. "Sir," he said respectfully, "we have Lawton. We took him from the guardhouse because we agree with him. It is now three months since we were paid. We want pay."

The captain pulled himself up to his full height. He uttered three words which shook Anne to the roots of her being. "This is mutiny!"

The man on the path stood at attention. "Our pay has been so long delayed, sir," he said. "We must have pay."

"Give me back my prisoner, and we will discuss the matter," the captain ordered.

"No, sir. We cannot do that."

"Stack arms," the captain said, "and then we will discuss it."

"No, sir, we cannot do that, either. But if you cannot tell how many we are because of the darkness, I would inform you that we are twenty."

"Half my garrison!" the captain exclaimed.

"If an alarm comes," the man went on in a matter-of-fact voice, "who will be at the alarm posts?"

There was a murmur from the men beyond the sentry. Anne wondered wildly whether Joel or any of her friends were there. Surely, she thought, they would not be party to a mutiny.

Captain Potter spoke angrily. "Have you forgotten the words

in your entitlement papers: 'I hereby promise to obey all such orders as I shall receive from time to time from my officers'?"

There was no response to this. Then the man on the path said, "We must have pay."

Captain Potter stood stiff as a poker, then he slumped. "Give me a moment."

He and his two lieutenants went into his office. Anne stood in the hall looking out at the now ominously quiet group of men. The man on the path did not stir. He stood like a ramrod, his eyes fixed on the doorway.

The captain came out of his office and strode to the door. A murmur went through the crowd at the sight of him. He held up his hand for silence. "If you go back to quarters and deliver Lawton over to the guards, I shall honor your requests without punishment. But Lawton is a thief. I will not let him go."

He pressed on, since the men seemed to be listening. "Surely you can understand that lawlessness cannot go unpunished in a military camp. Lawton must be punished for assault and for attempted theft. If you do not surrender my prisoner, there is no basis for discussion."

The man on the path turned and walked back to his friends. There was a consultation. He came back up the path. "If we deliver Lawton to the guards and go back to quarters, when will we receive our pay?"

"I will ride to Providence tomorrow and explain the urgency to the Council of War and to General Spencer, in command of the military affairs of this state. The Government has not forgotten you," he said, "but funds have been scarce. Deliver Lawton, march to quarters, and I will see that the paymaster comes to Warwick Neck tomorrow."

There was a pause while Anne held her breath. Then the group broke apart, there was a scuffle, and a man was thrust forward. The sentry stepped out and secured him. The group of men formed, turned, and marched off into the night. The captain, lieutenants, and Anne watched them go. They also watched the sentry march toward the guardhouse with his prisoner.

Slowly Captain Potter closed the door. He turned to his staff. "The devil!" he exclaimed. "A fine night's work!"

Slowly they climbed the stairs to their chambers. Anne snuffed out the candles she had lighted and again lay down to sleep, but sleep had left her. Through her head there echoed and re-echoed the words: "Not just for pay and rations, but to secure liberty and our independence." These men seemed to have forgotten that.

She lay all night thinking of that and of mutiny and wondering if her friends could have been among the men.

On the parade ground the next morning, all of the men looked alike. Anne could not tell the mutineers from the others.

She whispered to Joel, "There was a mutiny."

"I know," he whispered back, "but many of us were not there. We stayed in quarters."

Anne felt as if someone had taken a great weight from her shoulders. Joel had not put pay before the liberty of their country.

After roll call Lawton was brought forward and his sentence was read. He was then stripped to the waist and tied to a post. The drummer had to administer the lashes. He walked up to Lawton and raised the whip, which was made of several knotted cords. Anne choked back a scream when it came down on Lawton's back. She looked around at the men. They all watched grimly, for this was the usual punishment in the army.

Then Anne's eye was caught by Joel's face. It was drained of blood, his mouth was shut in a tight, thin line, a muscle twitched in his jaw. But he is a man, thought Anne, the rest of the men don't seem to mind, why should he?

It seemed to Anne as if the counting up to thirty was endless, as if the crack of the whip would sound across that parade ground forever. Part of her feeling was guilt because she had given evidence which had resulted in this whipping. Joel had, too, and she wondered if that was the reason he looked the way he did.

As they left the parade ground, she looked at him again. His face was still strained and his eyes . . . What was the expression in his eyes? she asked herself.

Later that day the paymaster arrived at the camp, but Anne could not share wholeheartedly in the joy of the other men. She was still distracted, haunted by the expression in Joel's eyes. It worried her for a long time afterward, until the day the British sloop drove the brig aground in the cove right below their fort.

Chapter Five

The coming of spring in the year of 1777 was marked not only by budding trees. It was also marked by British frigates and sloops of war which again patrolled the bay, for as the ice melted, releasing its grip on growing things, it thawed the British out of their winter moorings.

First, they came up as far as the town of Bristol and blew up an American row galley. Then they burned buildings on Prudence Island. Later Quonset and Point Judith on the mainland were attacked by foraging parties which had to be driven off.

Early one morning in April, Anne heard the drum beat to arms. Before the long roll of the drum had faded away, she ran to her alarm post in the fort with her musket and her cartridge box. Men streamed into the fort from all parts of the camp. Word had spread that two vessels were sailing toward Warwick Neck, a British sloop and an American brig. Like fire in dry brush, word leaped from man to man that the British sloop was trying to drive the brig aground in order to capture her.

At her post Anne stood on tiptoe, her musket resting on the breastworks. The day was foggy, but the fog seemed to be burning off, and slowly out of it on the water of the bay a vessel emerged, an American brig, and then another, a sloop of war flying a British flag. The sloop of war seemed to be crowding close to the brig, forcing her onto the shore.

"Our cannon ought to be fired!" cried Anne. "They could destroy the sloop."

The man next to her muttered, "What are the gunners doin', playin' draughts?"

From Anne's left a big man answered, "They'll strike the brig if they fire. Can't you see how close together the two vessels are? They're holdin' their fire a-purpose."

Anne could see now that a shot from the cannon could damage the brig as well as the British sloop. Nothing could be done except to wait. Breathlessly, they watched while the brig came closer and closer to shore in an effort to evade the British ship. Then the brig shuddered and stood still.

A few of the watchmen cried out, "She's grounded! Now they'll take her!"

Behind the grounded brig, the British sloop swung her bow slowly into the light breeze. While her crew deftly managed the sails, her anchor crashed into the water. Immediately her decks swarmed with men, and it looked as if they were trying to put boats over the side.

Soon a shot rang out from the British sloop, which was answered by muskets from the brig, but it was apparent to the men in the fort that the small crew of the American vessel could never stand up to an armed sloop. The British would board her and take her as a prize.

The officer in charge saw this, too. "Fix bayonets!" he ordered. "March to the shore!"

Anne clambered over the breastworks with the men. For an instant she felt a powerful surge of elation and a half-formed thought crossed her mind: now I am fighting for my country!

She scrambled down the bank with the men and ran along the shore. The officer in charge cast a shrewd eye at the distance between the shore and the grounded brig.

"Muskets and cartridge boxes over your heads," he shouted, "Forward, march!"

The men raised their muskets and cartridge boxes high over their heads and splashed into the surf. The water came up as high as Anne's chest by the time they reached the brig. Some members of the crew saw them approaching and threw lines over the side and stretched their arms down to help with the muskets. The soldiers climbed aboard, hand over hand up the ropes.

As Anne gained the deck, someone handed back her musket. There, for the first time, she smelled the acrid smoke of gunpowder, heard the scream of bullets.

No sooner had the last men pulled themselves over the gunwales than they were ordered to load their muskets, but before they had finished, Captain Potter shouted a warning. The swivel gun on the British sloop was leveled at the brig. Quickly Anne and the men scattered for cover, some behind the longboats, some crouched near the gunwales, some pressed against the side of the deckhouse.

Tense, Anne stood behind a mast. The gun was fired, but only flashed. Immediately Captain Potter gathered his men together. He ordered them to form on deck. "Aim for the gunners! Fire!" he shouted.

They fired. Anne set her teeth and braced herself for, in spite of the volley, the cannon on the sloop was leveled at them and fired again. This time the men held their places, and the ball passed above them and went through the sail of the brig.

As she rammed a bullet down the muzzle of her gun, Anne looked at the line of men. All were grim-faced, intent. One man was putting bullets into his mouth, one after the other, to have them ready when he needed them. The noise of ramming, of swearing, the whine of balls filled the air. Anne concentrated on loading her musket. She lost track of everything except the orders from Captain Potter and the Redcoats across on the deck of the sloop.

Once she and the others were ordered to hold their fire.

"Why?" she asked the man next to her.

"We only got what's in our cartridge boxes. Seventeen rounds," he said reasonably.

Oh, thought Anne, saving bullets. What will happen if we use up our bullets too soon? Are we at their mercy then?

Her answer came when the cannons at the fort were fired at last and were answered by the British. A furious cannonade began. The noise was deafening: smoke swirled about their heads.

Again the order came from their captain: "Fire!"

Anne fired, reloaded, rammed, fired until there seemed to be nothing else except her musket and the Redcoats at whom she aimed. To make the two connect was all there was in the world.

How long the encounter lasted Anne couldn't tell, but finally the crew on the sloop of war seemed to be making preparations to withdraw. Anne could see that some of the spars were cut through. One or two of their swivel guns must be useless, she thought, and perhaps we outnumber them now in muskets.

The British weighed anchor, hoisted what sail they could, and the sloop began to move away. A shot was fired from her deck as she slid off, but the ball passed under the stern of the brig. Then there was only scattered musket fire from the two vessels, and as the sloop drew farther away, Captain Potter ordered, "Hold your fire!"

Anne took a deep breath and sagged forward onto her gun. She had been so tense that now, with the danger past, she felt the strain. Her shoulder ached where the musket had kicked, her legs felt cramped, and her head pounded. With all the discomfort, though, she was elated. They had held the brig.

The men grinned at each other, black-faced, tired, proud men. Anne looked around her for Joel to share the joy of the victory with him, but she could not see him anywhere.

Can he be wounded? She thought in panic.

The captain strode toward them. "Well done," he said. "The crew will remain behind to guard the cargo of salt and to get their vessel off the sand bar. We will return to camp."

They slid down the lines and waded back to the shore, muskets again held high over their heads.

Anne's companions were in fine spirits. They shouted back and forth to each other.

Chapter Five

"She'll float off the sand bar at the turn of the tide," said one.

"She will if they unload her," said another.

"She will anyway," said a third.

"No trouble about that," another agreed.

"How many Redcoats did we get?" a deep voice asked.

"Ten or fifteen," was the answer.

"More," someone said.

There was a moment of silence as they splashed over the rocks, then a new voice asked hesitantly, "How many dead have we?"

"None," came the answer.

This was contradicted by a sharp voice saying, "Two, I think."

Anne remained silent. "Two," he had said. Could one be Joel? She scanned the line of men for him but could not see him.

When they reached the shore they turned toward the camp, to the parade ground. There Captain Potter made a speech, but Anne didn't hear much of it. She kept looking around for Joel. Her mind and heart were concerned with him only. Where was he? What had happened to him? A few of the captain's words penetrated: "In the first affray with the enemy . . . defended the brig . . . loaded with a valuable cargo of salt . . . behaved like men and patriots . . . extra gill of rum . . . dismissed."

No one spoke now, they were too tired. They moved away quietly.

Anne walked to the farmhouse sick at heart at the thought of Joel missing, of Joel drowned, of Joel dead. She put away her coat and hat and musket and changed her wet breeches and stockings for dry ones. She had no other shoes, so she put the wet ones back on. She washed her face and discovered that the palms of her hands were burned by the rough hemp ropes of the brig. When she finished washing, she saw there was no water left, so she picked up a bucket and went to the well.

She had lowered the bucket when from behind shrubbery near the well a voice said, "Andy."

It was Joel!

Slowly he came out from the clump of bushes. He looked sick.

"What is it?" Anne asked. "Were you wounded?"

"No," said Joel softly. "I wasn't shot. I wasn't there."

"You weren't there?" Anne repeated. "But everyone was there, the whole company except for the gunners."

"I was not there," Joel repeated. "I knew you would miss me even though no one else would. I thought you might need me." He half-turned away from her. "Turned out, I needed you."

"Why do you need me?" Anne asked.

"I'm a coward, Andy," Joel said in a burst. "I'm a coward. I was so scared, I couldn't go down."

Anne looked at him.

"Yes," he said. "Tell me what you think of me."

Anne could only ask, "Were you not at your alarm post, either?"

"Yes," Joel answered. "I went there, but when the order came to go to the shore, I stayed behind."

Anne saw that he was trembling. She was shocked by the fact that he had disobeyed orders. She was touched because he had confided in her and yet . . . Oh, she thought, if only I could touch his dear face, if I could tell him my secret . . . if he could know I am a woman . . . who loves him. For a moment she was tempted to tell him, but she knew he cared for her only as a younger brother. If she were to tell him, then he would be lost to her, and her chance to fight for liberty would be lost, too.

"Say it," Joel cried, "say what you are thinking."

"I cannot, Joel," Anne answered truthfully. "Oh, Joel, I cannot."

"A young boy like you," he said, "follows orders and I . . . and I . . ." he choked.

Anne saw that he had had his punishment for his moment of weakness. The thoughts that had tortured him in the hours he had spent alone would stay with him forever. He had suffered.

"Go back to quarters," she said. "No one will have noticed. You can be sure of that."

Chapter Five

"You don't think so?" Joel asked like a little boy looking for reassurance.

To Anne their positions seemed reversed. She was acting the part of the older brother. He seemed the lad.

"I don't think so," she answered.

"You don't despise me?" he pleaded.

"I don't despise you."

"I despise myself," he muttered, and he turned and walked slowly away, his feet dragging, looking neither to the right nor to the left.

Anne pulled up a bucket of water and went back to the farmhouse. Disappointment welled up in her as she realized what Joel had done—or had not done. Her eyes were misted with tears. And yet, she thought fiercely, he cannot help it. It is the way he is. Not everyone is born to be a fighter.

She entered the kitchen. Mechanically she dipped water from the bucket into the kettle and hung the kettle on the crane in the fireplace. She sat on a stool staring into the fire.

The flames reminded her of the fire Joel had built in the sugar storehouse. Now Anne knew: he had been afraid that night and had built the fire to drive off possible attackers. He had not tripped on the parade ground as the company moved forward that morning; he had not wanted to volunteer. And the day Lawton had pushed his way in, he had been afraid then, too.

Oh, thought Anne, so many signs, but I saw none.

For a moment she seemed to see Joel's face as it had looked the day of Lawton's whipping and again as it had looked as he came out from behind the clump of shrubbery. The vision blurred as the tears in her eyes brimmed over. Angrily she dashed them away with the back of her hand. She got up from the stool.

Just the same, I love him, she thought. Perhaps because he is this way, I love him more—as if he were a child. In a moment of illumination, she knew that that must be part of every woman's love for a man, to see him at times as if he were a child.

When they met again, Joel didn't talk about his cowardice anymore, and neither did Anne. In the fine spring weather, when they had been dismissed for the day, they walked to the shore to watch the gulls; sometimes they dug clams. They paraded with the company, they maneuvered, they marched to the nearby church for divine services. Small things filled up the first part of the summer, and it was not much disturbed by the British. And Anne could not bear to disturb the peace that lay between them.

But two emotions filled her life: her love for Joel, and her desire to do her share in the war for independence. Which was the stronger, she could not tell. Her love had been tested by Joel's confession. It remained firm and steady. It grew stronger day by day because now she felt his need; she felt they were tied by the secret he had confided. In July a chance to test her patriotism came.

Chapter Six

One night during the first week in July there was a violent rainstorm. Anne was cooking Captain Potter's dinner, and the fire sputtered as rain dropped down the chimney. She was testing the chickens in the pot to see if they were tender when the kitchen door to the hall was thrust open. Lieutenant Smith stood there.

"Sands," he said, "set five more places, we have unexpected guests."

Five more places, thought Anne. I will have to add water to the broth and find something else to eat; the chickens will not be enough. She fetched dishes and tankards from the cupboard and set the table. It looked crowded, but it was the best she could do.

As she added more water to the pot, she heard a great commotion in the front hall, the sound of heavy boots and loud talking. Anne collected all the cheese and bread and cold meat she could find and put them on the table.

Soon Captain Potter put his head in the door. "Ready, Sands?" he asked.

"Yes, sir," Anne answered. She heard the men file into the dining room, and when she thought they were seated, she carried in the broth and the chickens. As she served, she noticed that one of the visitors was a colonel. He was a large man with dark hair, cropped close, and dark eyes. With him were four officers, a captain and three lieutenants. Captain Potter and his staff seemed to be listening to the colonel with great deference.

"When do you plan to start?" Captain Potter asked.

"As soon as the weather clears," the colonel replied. "We

should have gone tonight, but this storm will not end this night, I fear."

Anne stood just inside the kitchen door in order to be near if Captain Potter wanted her. She wondered what important expedition was about to take place. She hoped it was something exciting, for certainly things had been as quiet at this army fort as at Brownes' Mill.

The colonel leaned toward Captain Potter. "I am short a man," he confided. "Last evening from Bristol I took my men over to Hog Island. We could see the whole British fleet riding at anchor out there, and that is where I disclosed my plan to them. We went back to Bristol full of enthusiasm, but this morning one of my men awoke with such ague in his face that I left him behind. Have you a man who could take his place?"

Anne became excited. I would like to take his place, she thought. Do I dare? How shall I say it? Now? Or later to Captain Potter?

"Sands!" The name shattered her thoughts and brought her into the dining room with a "Yes, sir?"

"Bring some ale."

"Yes, sir," said Anne. She fetched the pitcher of ale and filled the tankards. In her anxiety about whether to speak or not, she clumsily spilled some on the table at the colonel's place. He looked up at her. She felt herself blush, then blurted out, "I heard, sir, that you needed another man. I would gladly go."

"Sands!" Captain Potter's voice was firm. "You forget yourself."

"Yes, sir," said Anne, subsiding.

The colonel said, "But Potter, it is a fine idea not to have to ask the whole company for one volunteer. News of the expedition could leak out that way. This lad looks fit and alert and eager. Will you not let him come?"

Anne stood breathlessly waiting for Captain Potter's answer. He took a sip of his ale, put down his tankard, wiped his mouth,

Chapter Six

and said, "If you think so, Colonel, of course. But I give you the best cook and waiter I ever had."

Quickly Anne removed the plates. As she took the colonel's he said to her, "Tomorrow evening, if the storm has stopped, report to the beach below the fort at eight o'clock."

"Yes, sir. Thank you, sir," Anne said.

The next day toward noon the rain stopped and soon after that the clouds lifted. All afternoon Anne wondered where they could be going and for what. But she had no information until that night.

At eight o'clock, Captain Potter summoned her. "Leave your musket behind," he said. "You will not need it. The colonel's name is Barton. He is in charge of the expedition."

When Anne reached the meeting place she found a large group of men already assembled. Five whaleboats were lined up on the beach. Colonel Barton and his staff were there, too. When all the men were present, Colonel Barton stepped into the midst of them.

He spoke quietly and Anne had to strain to hear. "As I explained to you," he began, "we are going to row to the northern part of the island at Newport, and there we are going to capture Major General Richard Prescott, British commander of forces in this state."

He held up his hand for silence, and the cries of delight were choked back. "Now count off," he directed, "so that everyone has a number."

The men began, "One. Two. Three." Anne was thirty-three. There were forty men besides Colonel Barton.

Pointing to a man who stood near him, Colonel Barton said, "Hall, here, was raised on the island. He will lead us from the landing spot to headquarters. I will be in the first boat with a handkerchief tied to a pole so that you will be able to see to follow. Five men, numbers eight, sixteen, twenty-four, thirty-two, and forty will stay with the boats when we land.

One man to each whaleboat as a guard. We will break up into five groups, seven men to each. Groups one, two, and three, will attack the three doors of the house. Four will guard the road. Five will stand ready for any emergencies. Are there any questions?"

There was silence. There were no questions.

In a low voice the colonel added, "You are all to preserve the strictest order. There is to be no plundering, and you are to observe absolute silence. The oars are muffled?" He turned to one of his officers.

"Yes, sir," he replied.

Colonel Barton said, "We are ready then." He paused. "May God protect us and bless this expedition with success."

All the men and Anne removed their hats. "Amen," they murmured.

They turned to the boats, and Anne got into the fifth one. As they pushed off, she noticed that the stars were shining but that it was the dark of the moon. That suited their purpose. She was excited and a little frightened, for now she knew this was a dangerous expedition. She peered ahead to see the first boat with the handkerchief tied to a pole. She could just barely make it out.

With muffled oars they rowed between Prudence and Patience Islands. Down the west side of Prudence they went and around its southern tip. There they saw a British frigate lying off the shore. They passed so close to it that they heard the sentinel on deck call, "All is well!" Anne hardly dared to breath as they rowed by, but they passed undetected, and soon they were nearing the island of Newport. Steadily up ahead the handkerchief gleamed white on Colonel Barton's pole. Silently the whaleboats followed. No one spoke.

Soon they were pulling the boats up onto a beach. Quietly the men formed into the five groups and marched forward. In a moment they were walking through a gully full of scratchy bushes. When they emerged from the gully, they crossed some

Chapter Six

meadows, and after they had walked about a mile, they were ordered to halt.

Three groups were sent to attack the doors of the house on the south, east, and west. Anne was in the fifth group, the one to act as circumstances required. This was Colonel Barton's. Anne could now make out what looked like a small guardhouse on their left.

A British sentry called out, "Who goes there?"

"Friends," said Colonel Barton, and gave the signal to the man he had called Hall. Hall crawled off across the space between the men and the guardhouse. All the Americans had frozen, had become voiceless statues.

Again the sentry's voice demanded, "Give the countersign."

Colonel Barton answered, "We have no countersign to give. Have you seen any deserters tonight?"

The sentry didn't answer. He couldn't. Hall had approached him in the dark and had secured him and put one hand over his mouth.

Now Colonel Barton went closer. "Is General Prescott in the house?" he asked.

The sentry nodded. He seemed terrified.

At his answer the fifth group left the fourth to guard the road and marched on, up an avenue lined with trees.

Anne could now make out the forms of men approaching the house from the three directions: south, east, and west. Quickly they forced the doors. Her group entered and fanned out through the house, looking for General Prescott's chamber. It was dark, and they didn't know where to turn until an old man's voice called out, "Barrington! Barrington!"

The call came from a chamber at the rear of the house. Colonel Barton entered it. The fifth group stood at the door, waiting for any trouble.

A candle flickered on a table, throwing a dim light over a little old man sitting up in bed.

Colonel Barton asked, "Are you General Prescott?"

"I am," the man answered.

"In the name of the United States of America, I order you to surrender!"

General Prescott reached for a gold watch that hung on the wall by the bed.

"Do not move," warned Colonel Barton quickly.

General Prescott looked small and feeble. He said, "I surrender."

One of Colonel Barton's lieutenants stepped forward and picked up the general's clothes from a chair.

"May I get dressed?" asked Prescott.

"There is not time now," said Colonel Barton. He picked up another garment. "Here is a cloak. Put that around you. We will take your coat and breeches."

There was a sudden loud commotion down the hall. Anne and the rest ran, and saw a British soldier just disappearing through a window. Two men dived after the Redcoat. Anne and the others ran out the door and around the corner of the house. In the shrubbery they pounced on him. He struggled.

"Let me go," he cried. "I am General Prescott's aide!"

They pinioned his arms and walked him back to the door. Colonel Barton was just emerging with General Prescott. The men gathered from the other doors and from the road. "Back to the boats," ordered the colonel. "I want General Prescott carried so that we can make better time. Has someone the sentry?"

"Yes, sir," came a voice.

Anne looked. Hall had the sentry.

"And an aide-de-camp," came another voice.

"Proceed in a trot," ordered Colonel Barton.

Across the fields they dashed and into the gully to the shore. Branches slashed and cut them as they tore through. Near the boats Colonel Barton handed General Prescott his clothes.

"Be quick in your dressing," he ordered.

Chapter Six

The men were in their places at the oars, all of them breathing hard from running and from the excitement. General Prescott, his aide, and the sentry were with the colonel in his boat.

"You are to observe perfect silence," Colonel Barton warned the prisoners in a whisper, "or it will go hard with you. Do you understand?"

They nodded.

The boats were pushed off and, silent as shadows, they left the island that was occupied by the British. Around the southern tip of Prudence Island they rowed, again passing close to the British frigate. Between Patience and Prudence softly, swiftly they plied the oars with eyes fastened on the white handkerchief up ahead. Every man was ready to shout with joy for the success of the expedition, but the moment for shouting had not yet arrived. They might still be discovered. An alarm could still be given.

Land loomed ahead. Was that Warwick Neck? thought Anne. She could hardly believe they were back so soon.

As they landed, she heard General Prescott ask, "Are you in command?" He addressed Colonel Barton.

"I am," the colonel replied.

"Sir," said Prescott, "you have made a bold push tonight."

"Sir," answered Colonel Barton, "we have been very fortunate."

"You do not mean to kill me?" asked General Prescott.

"We do not, sir. You have no personal injury to fear."

Colonel Barton then ordered the men and prisoners to march to the farmhouse.

Captain Porter greeted them. "What luck, sir?" he called out.

Colonel Barton, as if he were presenting new arrivals to a host, said, "Here is General Prescott, and here—" He stopped.

The aide-de-camp said, "Barrington, Major Barrington."

"Major Barrington," said the colonel. "General Prescott's aide-de-camp. And here—" He stopped again.

The sentry muttered, "Graham."

"And Graham, a sentry," concluded Colonel Barton. His voice changed, became brisker and more military. "Please send an express to Major General Spencer at Providence and ask him for a coach and a guard for General Prescott."

Captain Potter nodded. "Yes, sir," he said.

Colonel Barton turned to his men. "We have dared much," he said, "and we have won much. I thank you all."

The men cheered him again and again, in this way giving expression to their excitement, their love for Colonel Barton, and their joy at their success.

"Rum all around," said the colonel, "and then we shall start for Tiverton." He turned to Captain Potter again. "I would advise you to take the prisoners to the nearest tavern and hold them there until the coach and guard arrive from Providence."

"Yes, sir," said Captain Potter. "The express will go off immediately. I will follow your orders."

Rum was handed out. Anne stood back; she never took her ration of rum. She noticed now that day was breaking, the blackness was just turning to gray. Colonel Barton must have noticed it, too, for he gathered his men together and, after a final word with Captain Potter, they departed.

Guards came and marched the prisoners off down the road to the nearest tavern. Anne stood at the door of the farmhouse and watched them leave. Then she snuffed out the candles and fell on her sack, tired but exhilarated by her share in the capture of the British general.

That morning, when the men paraded, the officer of the day told them the story of the capture of Prescott, and Anne felt as proud as a peacock. Later, a boat bearing a flag of truce arrived at Warwick Neck, bringing the general's wardrobe, his money, his hair powder, and his body servant. Again the camp buzzed with talk about the expedition. Anne told Joel then about her share in it.

"Weren't you afraid?" he asked.

"Yes," Anne answered, "I was fearful at times, but also excited and proud to be there."

"You are a true patriot, Andy," said Joel, and clapped her on the shoulder.

Anne's face shone with pride and joy and some of this feeling must have stirred in his breast, too, for he said, "Andy, if ever you hear of another expedition, volunteer my services, will you?"

"I will," Anne promised.

And with these two words, Anne sealed Joel's fate—and her own.

Chapter Seven

One day early in the fall, when Anne came into Captain Potter's office to work, she was surprised to find the whole staff assembled. The men seemed troubled and were talking earnestly with their heads together. Anne stood for a moment, not knowing what to do, but Captain Potter, looking up, saw her and ordered her to come closer.

"You have had experience in secret expeditions," he said. "Will you go on another?"

"Yes, sir," Anne said eagerly, gladly. Her heart thumped. Here was a chance to offer Joel's service, too. "And so will any of the men," she added, "especially Joel Sherman. He is most anxious to go."

"Sherman?" the captain repeated. "Oh, yes, a friend of yours?"

"Yes, sir."

Captain Potter wrote: Sands. Sherman. "That's two," he said. "About a dozen, would you say?"

His lieutenants nodded.

"We will get ten others from the company. And, Smith, you will lead it?"

"Yes, sir," Lieutenant Smith answered.

Captain Potter turned to Anne. "Sands, I have a dispatch to send to General John Spencer. Come back in a few minutes. I will have it ready then."

"Yes, sir," said Anne. She felt pleased with herself for having suggested Joel. Now he would see that it was possible to forget oneself while serving one's country. Perhaps soon all would be well with him.

Chapter Seven

All except the fact that he thinks I am a lad, thought Anne. This she found harder and harder to bear lately. More than once she was sorely tempted to give herself away. The only thing that prevented her from doing so was her ardent wish to serve her country further, to help drive the enemy from their shores.

When she returned to copy the dispatch, she found out that it concerned a deserter from the British Army. He had come into their camp early that morning and had volunteered the information that a British frigate would land at the north end of Prudence Island in three nights to take on a supply of water.

Oh, thought Anne, then the expedition will be to Prudence Island, to catch the landing party.

She was right. With Joel and ten others, she met with Captain Potter and Lieutenant Smith the next day.

Captain Potter told them about the information they had received from the deserter. "We are going to send you over in the evening," he explained. "Lieutenant Smith will be in charge. The boats will be brought back. You will cover your tracks on the beach and hide out all night in the thicket on the knoll above the spring. We feel sure they will be taking their water from Indian Spring since that is the largest spring on the island. They will most assuredly arrive before dawn when they think our camp here across the cove is asleep. You will wait until the landing party has approached the spring. You are to obey Lieutenant Smith's commands to the letter. Everything depends on surprise."

As they left the meeting, Anne noticed that Joel looked strained. She smiled at him reassuringly. "I shall be an expert in secret expeditions before this war is won."

He smiled, and they parted.

A few nights later Anne and the men chosen left Warwick Neck by boat carrying their muskets, knapsacks, and cartridge boxes.

The tide was coming in when they landed on Prudence Island. The men rowing the boats started back immediately, and Lieutenant Smith issued his first order.

"Do not move from the wet sand until I return," he said.

He and two men walked back from the water's edge, up a rise covered with shrubs. They returned in a few minutes with branches they had cut. They handed one to each man. "About face," ordered Lieutenant Smith. "Back up the beach, sweeping your footsteps from the dry sand as you go."

Anne took her branch and brushed the sand each time she took a step backward. Their footsteps on the wet beach would be washed away, she knew, but this was a good precautionary measure until the tide came in. Soon they all reached the top of the knoll.

"Thrust the branches into the earth so that they look like growing bushes," said Lieutenant Smith.

They did. Anne admired this plan. She said so to Joel. "They have thought of everything." He nodded.

They made their way through the shrubbery for a short distance along the top of the knoll until the sound of running water came to them. The Indian Spring, thought Anne. She was right. It was down there in a gully on the inner side of the knoll.

Lieutenant Smith stopped. "This is the place," he said. "They will approach from the other side of the island to this spring. We will wait until they are busy filling their casks before we fire. If, for any reason, they approach from the same direction as us, we will still surprise them, for we are on a knoll, hidden, and they will be on a beach, exposed. You may eat whatever you brought in your knapsacks and drink and talk in low voices for a few hours. No fires. No pipes."

The men, who had been standing rigidly at attention listening, now settled down on the ground. Some ate. Some talked. Joel sat near Anne.

As the night wore away, dew settled and the air was chilly. Knapsacks were put to one side. Tension mounted. Talk grew more and more half hearted, then stopped altogether. Guns were loaded at Lieutenant Smith's order and bayonets fixed.

Finally, at the first glimmer of dawn, they saw sails over the tops of the trees on the far side of the spring.

Lieutenant Smith spoke. "Everyone ready," he said. "No ramming of guns from now on. No talking. Do not move about too much lest the sound of crackling branches carry to them. No one is to fire except on my signal. No one must give our position away by any movement or sound. Is that clear?"

"Yes, sir," the men murmured.

They fell into position, some squatting, some lying flat on the ground. Joel and Anne were side by side.

"When I give the signal," Lieutenant Smith continued, "which will be my hand raised then dropped, I want a volley, then you are to charge down the knoll."

Now silence fell. The men lay waiting for what seemed an endless time, tense, cramped, uncomfortable. At last they heard the crackling of underbrush, and then from the shrubbery on the far side of the spring four Redcoats advanced with muskets poised. Immediately the atmosphere on the knoll became charged with tension. The Redcoats walked around the spring, peered into the bushes, climbed the rocks over which the water cascaded. When they were satisfied that there was no danger, one man went back, presumably to tell the others. Soon the full party approached, about fifteen men, several of whom rolled casks for the water. Some of the men formed a loose circle around the spring, while others within the circle began to move the casks to the water for filling.

At that moment Joel's musket slipped out of his hands, and the barrel of it struck a rock. Metal on rock resounded sharp and loud across the hollow, and the Redcoats looked up in alarm.

Lieutenant Smith crawled up to Joel. "Fool!" he hissed. "You gave us away." He raised his hand, then dropped it.

It was the signal.

The volley sounded like thunder across the gully.

"Charge!" commanded Lieutenant Smith.

The men rose and dashed out of the thicket. Anne ran forward with the rest toward the Redcoats. One was standing in her path at the bottom of the knoll. He seemed to be coming to meet her, but she felt no fear. Suddenly she felt a rush of air, and Joel was running at her side, and at the moment she realized that it was Joel the Redcoat meant to kill. Joel must have seen it, too. He reached out and grabbed Anne and, with great strength, pulled her over and held her in front of him as a shield against the Redcoat.

Then everything happened at once. Instantaneously, it seemed to Anne, Joel collapsed and pulled her down with him. At the same moment there was a sharp pain in her thigh. She and Joel rolled down the rest of the knoll and came to rest at the bottom. Anne could hear the British soldier panting and cursing her and Joel and shouting to someone as he ran off, "They're both dead!"

Anne pretended to be unconscious for a few moments, then cautiously she opened her eyes. The searing pain in her thigh was almost unbearable. Had she been wounded with a bayonet or by a bullet? She didn't look to find out. Instead, she raised her head and stared at Joel. There was a bullet hole in his forehead, and his face still wore an expression of terror. She reached out and picked up his hand and let it go. It fell to the ground, lifeless.

She cried out in her grief, but when the memory of what he had done returned, she recoiled from him. "Oh, Joel!" she said out loud. "Oh, Joel!" and put her head down on the ground and wept. She had loved him, and he—he had tried to use her as a shield to sacrifice her life to save his own.

She realized now that he had cared nothing for her. Tears streamed down her face; sobs shook her body. For a few moments she cried uncontrollably, forgetting everything but her grief and disillusionment. Then the shouts of men still fighting became insistent. She raised her head again and looked around.

Chapter Seven

Over at the spring all the men were in a knot, fighting hand to hand. Anne could not reach her own cartridge box, but she could reach Joel's. She took out bullet and powder and tried to load her musket, but she could not do it. The effort exhausted her, and she lay back. From moving about, one leg of her breeches had become soaked with blood. As the minutes went by, she felt weaker, and she must have fainted, for the next thing she knew someone dashed water on her face, and someone else said, "Sherman is dead."

"And Sands?" asked another voice.

Anne felt a hand touch her shoulder as if to raise her from the ground. She became terror-stricken. She hadn't known such fear since the beginning of her disguise as a boy. "I'm alive," she said quickly.

"How badly are you hurt, Sands?" asked Lieutenant Smith.

"Only a flesh wound," Anne lied. "I will attend to it. It bled so much, sir. That must be why I fainted."

Two men helped her up. She put her arms around their necks, and they half-carried her to the beach. Once she looked back at Joel's body. "He will be buried where he fell," one of her companions said.

"Just as well," she answered, and those were the last words she said until they got her to the beach.

She had no strength for talking. Every bit of her strength went into the effort to stay conscious with the acute pain in her leg.

When they reached the beach they lay down and waited for the boats. It was still not full daylight. Again someone offered to look at her wound, but she refused. She lay there silently grieving over Joel, sick with the thought of what he had done. She was in pain and fearful to be with these men now that she was wounded, helpless, incapable of walking by herself.

As soon as the boats came, they lifted her into one, and at Warwick Neck somehow they got her out of it and up to the farmhouse. There they left her, and in the privacy of the kitchen, Anne slashed off the leg of her breeches and looked at the hole in her thigh. The bullet lay embedded in the flesh. She probed for it, but couldn't get it, so she washed out the wound, bound it up, found her second pair of breeches, put them on, and lay down on her sack.

Then, in the stillness, like a stream of water falling over her, there poured the bitter memory of Joel, of how, with brute strength, he had pulled her in front of him to protect his life. I meant nothing to him, she thought. He said I was his younger brother, that he loved his younger brother, but he loved no one except himself. Anne turned her face into her arms to smother her sobs.

When Captain Potter found no breakfast ready, he stamped angrily into the kitchen calling, "Sands!"

Anne raised her head. "I am sorry, sir," she said. "I was wounded on Prudence."

Immediately Captain Potter's mood changed. "A doctor is coming from Providence today to administer smallpox inoculations to some men," he said. "He will look at your wound."

"No," said Anne, alarmed. "I mean, no, sir. It is not a bad wound. I will dress it myself. But I am afraid, sir, that I cannot go to assembly or cook."

"No matter," said Captain Potter. "I will eat with some of the men and bring you some food, too."

"I do not care for any," said Anne. She sank back, exhausted.

Late in the day Anne managed to get up and dress the wound again. Gritting her teeth, she probed for the musket ball, but she could not get it. She felt very sick.

I wonder, she thought, if I should find the house where the inoculations are being given and tell the doctor who I am. She was tempted, but she felt as if she did not have the strength. She fell back onto her sack.

That night she began to feel feverish. Things took on odd shapes and shifted back and forth. She was parched with thirst. The next morning, she determined to see the doctor. Outside, she

Chapter Seven

found a thick stick in the woodpile, the paling of a fence. With the help of this, she got to the parade ground and could answer the roll. She stood there, swaying with the waves of pain, while some announcements were read: one about the inoculations, one about the surrender of the British General Burgoyne at Saratoga with more than five thousand men! This meant, without a doubt, that the war soon would be over. She also heard that Rhode Island forces from all the camps around the bay were gathering at a place called Tiverton for an attempt to dislodge the British from Newport, and that men from their camp would march there soon, too. Oh, thought Anne, the end is in sight!

After assembly she refused all offers of assistance and hobbled slowly down the road that led to the house where the inoculations were being given. She decided that when she reached the house, she would wait at the door until some time when the doctor would be alone. Every step cost her dearly, for now the sensation of fire had moved up and down her leg. She was in agony. When she was still a way from the farmhouse, she saw a man she thought must be the doctor come out of the door and walk toward a horse tied to a tree.

Oh, thought Anne, he must not go now. I'm so close. Panic seized her. She screamed, ran a few steps, and then everything turned black.

When she regained consciousness, she was lying on the ground, and a gray-haired man with a kind face was cutting away the leg of her breeches. She started up in alarm. "No!" she cried. "Please! No!"

"Lie down, madam," he ordered her sternly, but clearly, so that she would understand.

Anne looked at him, startled, frightened at his words. "How did you . . . ?" she began.

"I am a doctor," he said quickly. "I examined you and found you to be a female soldier, and a brave one at that. When did you get this bullet in your thigh?"

"Yesterday. The day before," said Anne. "It runs together in my head." She shook her head as if to shake things into focus. "On Prudence Island," she began again. "We crossed over to surprise a party of Redcoats."

"You did," said the doctor. "You killed three and wounded five. Only one of your party was killed."

"I know," said Anne. Her lips set in a firm line.

"A friend of yours?" asked the doctor.

Anne shook her head in denial. "No friend of mine," she said bitterly, and the tears welled up and spilled over. She dashed them away with her hand.

"I am going to take you to Providence," said the doctor. "This camp is no place for a sick female. I must operate on this leg. You will be sicker before you are well. I am Dr. Cooper."

"And I am Andy Sands," said Anne automatically. "Or really," she added, as he looked at her with eyebrows raised, "Anne Saunders."

He had re-bandaged her leg deftly. He packed up his things. "I will notify the officer in charge here," he said. "The ride back will not be pleasant. I do not have a carriage, and you will have to ride pillion on my horse." He stood up. "Ready, Miss Saunders?"

"I cannot go to Tiverton with the men?" Anne pleaded.

"No, you cannot," the doctor answered firmly. "Your fighting days are over."

But the doctor was wrong. Anne's fighting days had just begun. This fight, though, was not for her country. It was for her life.

Chapter Eight

The ride to Providence was a nightmare. Anne was conscious part of the time, but mostly she was not. Dr. Cooper's firm hand and arm kept her on the horse. His kind words of encouragement prevented her from screaming out, for the movement of the horse intensified the pain.

For much of the time she didn't care whether they ever got to Providence. She would have preferred to be left at the side of the road and forgotten. It is too hard, she thought. The jogging of the horse is more than I can bear.

Toward the end of the ride, it seemed to her that a kind of mist separated her from everything else. She couldn't see or feel it or hear clearly, either.

And then, at last, she was not on horseback any longer. She felt strong hands lifting her down. She was near a fire; it was warm. A woman was there. Is that really a woman? thought Anne. How long since I have seen a woman? She tried to say something but couldn't.

She felt the woman's hands, gentle hands, undress her, bathe her, put a soft garment on her, lift her into bed. Anne felt herself sinking, sinking into the wonderful softness of that bed. Then something was forced to her lips, something that burned until the burning inside her equaled the burning, throbbing fire in her leg.

Later she felt even greater pain, and she screamed, whereupon the woman's voice said gently, "There, there. Dr. Cooper has the bullet. It is all over. Now you can sleep."

But there was no real sleep for Anne. When she felt she might be on the verge of falling asleep, she would remember the happenings on Prudence Island and start up in fright.

Gently they made her lie down and gave her a sip of cool water, bathed her, and said, "Sleep, my dear, sleep."

She tried to sleep, but in a half-waking, half-sleeping moment, she would see the fire over which Joel had cooked the rabbit. For a moment it would be Joel's fire, then it would be Sam's fire in the blacksmith shop with Sam's face bending over it while he made a bayonet.

Over and over in her delirium these pictures whirled and turned and chased each other through Anne's brain, and always she burned with fever, and her leg throbbed and pained.

At last there came a day, though, as Anne lay in bed, when the pain diminished, the fever subsided, and she was filled with a great quietness and peace.

She lay there not stirring. Slowly, carefully, with great effort she opened her eyes. They fell on a mantel, then dropped to the fire burning below. She moved her head bit by bit to one side. A chair stood near the bed, and sitting in it was a beautiful woman. She had grayish hair with a ruffled cap on it, pink cheeks, clear blue eyes. The sunlight poured into the room behind her so that she seemed to be sitting in a pool of light. She smiled.

"Good morning," she said as if she loved the morning. "You slept well."

Anne nodded. She couldn't seem to speak. She was anxious, though. Who was this woman? Was this the same day?

The woman seemed to read her thoughts. "I'm Dr. Cooper's wife," she said. "He brought you here. He operated on your leg, and I have been taking care of you. You have been very sick. This morning you looked at me for the first time as if you knew I was a woman. Now it is almost midnight. Are you thirsty?"

Anne nodded.

Mrs. Cooper fed her something. As she took the spoon away from Anne's lips, she said, "Now you will get well. Would you like to know how long you have been here?"

Chapter Eight

Anne nodded again. It seemed to be all she had the strength to do.

"Almost a week," said Mrs. Cooper. "We were not sure you would get well until today. Now we know you will. I am happy about that, my dear. You are a brave girl."

Tears welled up in Anne's eyes at the words of praise.

"No, do not cry," said Mrs. Cooper. She sponged Anne's face gently. "Just go to sleep, if you please."

Like a child, Anne did as she was told. She slept quietly, coolly, dreamlessly. When she awoke the next morning she was alone. She raised her arm with a great deal of effort and looked at it. She was shocked by its thinness.

I must have been very sick, she thought. The sunlight poured in the window and was reflected off a brass warming pan near the fireplace and a shiny pewter candlestick on the table near the bed.

Anne smiled to see the candlestick. It is like the one in my room at Brownes' Mill, she thought. My room. I am not the same person who left that room. How long ago?

She thought of all that had come between then and now. The war. The talk with Sam. Her enlistment. Joel. The camp. Her wound. All of it seemed to stand out in her mind as clearly as things in the room did in the bright light of the morning. Only the word "Joel" made her heart ache. I must not dwell on him if I want to get well, she thought, and now, this sunny morning, she knew she wanted to.

That was the turning point in Anne's illness. Each day after that she became stronger. Soon she sat up, and it seemed strange to see things from a sitting posture, for she had been lying down for so long. After that she limped about the room. When she had been sitting and walking for a few days, she became aware of the world outside her windows: a town with carts, horses, children, men, and women, and always soldiers marching to the sound of fifes and drums. The doctor had left with some troops, but Mrs. Cooper was always there.

One day Anne's heart was so full of gratitude that she said, "Mrs. Cooper, how shall I ever repay you for all you have done?"

"We want no repayment, Anne," Mrs. Cooper replied. "Just that you get well. Just so that you take up your life again when you are well enough."

"I would like to stay here with you forever," Anne burst out.

"And we would like to have you," Mrs. Cooper assured her, "for we never had a daughter. But you must have kinfolk of your own somewhere."

"I have no parents," Anne said, and told how her aunt had sent her to the Brownes' when she was ten. She told about the school, and then she added quickly, "That was an idea of Sam Prentice, the blacksmith at Brownes' Mill. Once he wanted me to be his wife."

"Perhaps he still does. Why did you not marry him?" Mrs. Cooper asked.

"I wanted to fight for the United States. I wanted more than Brownes' Mill. I wanted excitement and the world!"

"Oh, my dear," exclaimed Mrs. Cooper, "the world is where your happiness is."

Anne remained silent, astounded at the sudden realization that had come to her with Mrs. Cooper's words. Brownes' Mill and Sam had been in her thoughts constantly of late.

Deliberately then she thought of Joel. He seemed shadowy at first, but as the memory became clearer, there was a prick of the old hurt at what he had done to her.

Quickly she said, "Mrs. Cooper, I did not tell you about Joel, did I?"

Mrs. Cooper shook her head. "No," she said, "but you called out his name many times in your delirium."

Then, like a dam breaking, Anne told everything: how she had met him, how impressed she was with his manners, his ways, his talk, his looks. She told about his cowardice, about her love for him and how, at the end, he had used her. Words poured from her, all the feelings of all the months.

Mrs. Cooper listened, and when Anne had finished, she smiled and said, "I am pleased that you told me, Anne. I am sorry you had the experience, but it has not injured you. You will be better for it. You came away from home to search for something. You were looking for something as a person looks for a lost coin. He thinks anything that glints is the coin. You mistook Joel for the thing you were looking for, didn't you?"

"Yes," said Anne slowly, thinking it over, "that is the way it was. I was looking for something, and so I thought I had found it." She added in a soft voice, "Perhaps all the time it was at Brownes' Mill."

Mrs. Cooper smiled. "You can go back and claim it, Anne."

Anne looked at her, startled, and a picture of Sam flashed across her mind. If Joel seemed shadowy, Sam was real enough. Anne remembered his kindness, his love for her, his quiet ways. "The world is where your happiness is," Mrs. Cooper had said. Anne thought she knew now where that was.

She sat musing until she was brought back to the present moment by Mrs. Cooper's voice asking, "Why do you not go back to Brownes' Mill?"

"I am ashamed," Anne replied. "I think I would like to stay with you until after the war. I shall earn my keep from now on."

"I know you will," said Mrs. Cooper, "but you must not hide away with two old people. Why are you ashamed to go back to Brownes' Mill?"

"Because I treated Sam and the Brownes so badly. Because the Brownes lost their only son, and yet I left them. Because Sam loved me, and I left him."

"More reason to go back," said Mrs. Cooper. "Think about Brownes' Mill, Anne."

Anne did think about it, about the white houses around the common, about her school, about the Brownes, about the millpond, about Sam. All during that hard winter she thought about it. Through the sounds of fifes and drums and soldiers marching in the streets of the town. She thought and thought about it until she was filled with a longing to go back to Brownes' Mill.

One night she lay awake turning the problem over in her mind and listening to the night noises of the town: the crunch of carriage wheels on snow, a voice in the distance, a bell. The next morning there were dark shadows under her eyes.

"Are you well this morning?" asked Mrs. Cooper.

"Yes," Anne answered. "I lay awake a long time last night thinking I must return to help the Brownes. No," she said loudly, "that is not the truth!" She took a deep breath and laughed. "The truth is that I would like to go back to see Sam."

"Why do you laugh?" asked Mrs. Cooper.

"Because once I dressed as a lad, a fighting man looking for danger," Anne explained, "but I am a woman looking for love and a safe haven."

Mrs. Cooper seemed to understand. "When will you go then?"

"When the right time comes," Anne answered.

"But when will that be?"

"I cannot tell you, but I shall know it when it comes, and I shall be ready."

The next day, with the bounty money which Mrs. Cooper had found sewn in Anne's shirt when she was brought to the house, they purchased cloth and shoes. Together they sewed a gown and cloak. When the garments were finished, Anne put them away and waited for the right time.

One day in January, Mrs. Cooper was reading the Providence Gazette. She was feeling poorly and sat close to the fire. When Anne questioned her, she answered, "I have a chill. It is nothing, Anne." She turned the page of the newspaper and after a moment sighed.

Chapter Eight

"What is the matter?" Anne asked, concern in her voice.

"There is a notice here about the refugees from Newport. Listen." She read slowly: "'The charitable and well-disposed persons in this and the neighboring states are requested to extend their donations unto the poor and distressed people who were late inhabitants of Newport. Men and women bowed down with old age and infirmities, helpless children, and persons with large families have lately been driven from their once-peaceful habitations and turned into the wide world destitute of every means . . . Donations will be received at Joseph Clarke's . . .'" Mrs. Cooper stopped.

Oh, why did I spend my bounty money? thought Anne. I could have given it. I would have given it gladly.

Mrs. Cooper's voice cut through her thoughts. "Anne, we must gather together whatever food and clothing we can spare. I cannot leave the house. Do you feel strong enough to walk to the State House?"

"Yes," said Anne without hesitation.

Mrs. Cooper put down the newspaper and stood up. "Mr. Joseph Clarke," she explained, "is the Commissioner of the Loan Office. You will find him in the State House on Towne Street."

"Very well," Anne answered. "I will go, but I wish mightily that I had not spent my bounty money."

"You fought hard for that. You earned and deserved the things it bought. I have a good cheese and some biscuits, and there are some worn breeches and shirts of Dr. Cooper's."

A short while later Anne left the house carrying a large basket. She wore some of Mrs. Cooper's clothes: a market cloak and an old gown that Mrs. Cooper had given her when Anne felt well enough to be dressed. She still limped, so she walked carefully down the street. Footing was uncertain because there had been a sudden thaw, and slush and water were everywhere. Anne reached the Great Bridge and stood for a moment taking deep breaths of the cold air. The world looked exciting there across the water. There were masts and sails and the bustle of the wharves.

As she approached her destination, she noticed a man tying his horse to a hitching post, and instantly she recognized him. It was Sam Prentice! Anne's heart began to race. How fine he looks, she thought. She started to call to him, then stopped herself and stood shaking. No, she thought, I must not make myself known yet. Hastily, she crossed the street and stared into a silversmith's shop window. She put down her basket and pulled the hood of the cloak closer around her face. He must not see me so, she thought. He must not see me pale and limping and dressed in Mrs. Cooper's market cloak. He must not see me now.

She could not bear to leave the place, though, so she stood and stared at the few spoons and shoe buckles in the window and watched Sam's reflection. He took his saddlebags and carried them across the State House Parade.

Anne stood where she was, her mind filled with questions. What was Sam Prentice doing in Providence? Was he in the army? Did he remember that he had said he loved her? She watched him as he walked up the path. The same deliberate walk, she thought, unhurried but purposeful; like his life, there is a steady rhythm to it.

Sam disappeared into the State house, and Anne hugged herself inside the cloak. She felt miserable, on the verge of tears, as she waited there.

Soon she saw his reflection in the shop window coming back across the Parade. He buckled on his saddlebags, and at that moment, an intense emotion filled Anne's heart; a yearning so strong came over her to speak to him that she turned and put out her hand and opened her mouth to call his name, but the word "Sam" was never uttered, for he leaped into the saddle and rode off, looking neither to the right nor to the left, and Anne was left alone.

Chapter Eight

She stood motionless, for a moment, not quite believing that he had gone, staring at the spot where he had been, saying over and over to herself, "It is Sam I love. It is Sam!"

Then automatically, she picked up the basket, crossed the street, and walked up to the State House.

A man stood in the room just inside the door. "For the refugees?" he asked as Anne entered.

"Yes," she replied.

"Who has sent it?" he asked.

"Mrs. Cooper," Anne answered. "Dr. Cooper's wife."

"Are you kin of the Coopers?" he asked.

"No," said Anne. "Will you take the things out if you please, so that I can take the basket back?"

He began to take out the food and clothing. "This is the second large contribution this morning," he said. "A delegate to the General Assembly from Brownes' Mill, Mr. Prentice, was just here. He has been coming in with donations ever since the British landed in Newport a year ago."

Anne trembled. "A delegate to the General Assembly from Brownes' Mill?" she repeated. "He is not a soldier then?"

"He is more important than a soldier," the man answered. "He makes the best bayonets in this part of the country for the army."

That is just like him, thought Anne. Always the quiet things. Make the best bayonets. Be a delegate to the General Assembly. Bring donations to the refugees. "Oh, Sam," her heart cried out, "why could I not have seen what kind of man you were?"

After that day Anne became eager to return to Brownes' Mill. She realized that it had been a mistake to hide from Sam because she was still pale and thin, because she still limped. That does not matter, she thought. I want to see him. I want to speak to him!

She tried to make arrangements to leave Providence, but the snow was still wheel high on the roads, and stagecoaches were not making regular trips. Anne did not have a horse, and there was no prospect of borrowing one because most of the wagons and horses in Providence were being used by the army. Mrs. Cooper let it be known everywhere in town that Anne would be grateful for a ride if anyone were going toward Brownes' Mill. Anxiously, restlessly, Anne waited, and as the days and weeks went by, it seemed to her that no one would ever travel toward Brownes' Mill.

February passed slowly. March came. And by the end of March, she had a feeling of complete impatience, almost of desperation. She lived constantly with the thought: perhaps today I will be able to start out. She awoke hopeful each morning and fell asleep disappointed each night.

And then one day in April she heard the town crier out in the street. She opened the window and leaned out to hear what he was crying. It was exciting news of a treaty between the colonies and the country of France.

A treaty with France, thought Anne. Certainly now we will win the war!

Thirteen cannons roared from the battery on the hill and were answered by a growling of more cannons from the frigates in the harbor. A national salute, Anne thought. As if a signal had been given, the town seemed suddenly to come alive. It was a day for wild rejoicing. Below on the street the children shouted and pranced along after the town crier, and grownups gathered in knots to talk.

As Anne stood at the window, thinking about the end of the war and victory and peace, Mrs. Cooper entered the room. "Anne," she said excitedly, "everything happens at once. The treaty. You heard the crier? And a farmer has come with a load of firewood. He has brought it all the way from Southfield."

"Southfield," Anne repeated, and turned quickly from the window. "Why, that is just beyond Brownes' Mill!"

Mrs. Cooper nodded. "I know," she said simply.

Anne walked toward her. "Will he take me?" she asked.

Chapter Eight

Mrs. Cooper beamed. "I will see," she said. "If so, I shall make the arrangements." Her face became sober. "I will miss you, Anne," she said simply.

"I will miss you, too," Anne answered. "How shall I ever repay your kindness?"

"Pshaw!" said Mrs. Cooper. "I will go and talk to the farmer."

In this unexpected way, sixteen months after she left it, arrangements were made for Anne to return to Brownes' Mill.

Chapter Nine

Anne stepped into the street in front of the Coopers' house. It was cool for April, but everywhere there were signs of spring: the branches of the trees were feathery with buds, birds flew about carrying twigs and bits of straw, there was a faint fragrance in the air.

She stood for a moment, breathing deeply. Everything reborn, she thought, and I, too. Inside her cloak she ran a hand over her gown. It was so good to be dressed in women's clothes again, to be wearing a fine gown and shoes with buckles and a warm cloak. She hugged the cloak to her and turned to look at the house. Mrs. Cooper stood in the window waving. Anne waved, too, and slowly started down the street toward the Great Bridge. She carried a small box containing a few clothes and her honorable discharge from the army, which Dr. Cooper secured for her.

The farmer who had delivered the firewood to the doctor's house a few days before would be at the Market House about noon and would fetch her back to Brownes' Mill. Those were the arrangements she and Mrs. Cooper had made with him.

Anne hurried, for she was a bit late. She crossed the bridge and walked up to the Market House. She didn't see the farmer, and suddenly she felt weak with excitement. She leaned against a cart for a moment until the sensation passed, then walked around the Market House, from stall to stall, looking for him. Around and around she walked through the crowd of women and children and farmers. Finally she saw him and his wagon, waiting beside a mounting block. He put his finger to his hat and called down to her.

Chapter Nine

"Are you able to get aboard?" he asked.

"I will try," Anne said. She handed up her box, then scrambled up awkwardly. Not a very pretty sight, she thought, and smiled. I could have done better if I were wearing breeches.

"Ready?" asked the farmer.

"Ready," answered Anne, and pulled her cloak into place.

Away they drove out of Providence. It was a fairly long ride, and during it there were great periods of silence between them. Then again they would talk about the lack of food and wood and hay, about the British still in Newport, about the remarkable treaty America had just signed with France.

"It will bring us ships of war," said the farmer, "trained soldiers, gold, and supplies."

"You think then," asked Anne, "that France will help us win independence?"

"I am sure of it."

"And if Great Britain declares war on France?" she asked.

"Then we will support France, and neither of us will make peace without the consent of the other. We do not stand alone any longer, Miss Saunders. That is the remarkable fact. They have recognized us, the thirteen United States. The way will be easier from now on, and I, for one, can see only victory at the end."

Fervently Anne said, "I hope so. Oh, I hope so."

The nearer they came to Brownes' Mill, the faster and harder Anne's heart thumped. They passed the Dragon and finally, at the fork in the road near the church, she asked to be let down. She knew that the farmer was taking the other road at the fork, and, anyway, she preferred to walk into the town.

He handed her box down. She thanked him and was amazed when he thanked her.

"For what?" she asked.

"For fighting for us old ones, ma'am," he said.

"You know?" she asked.

"I do," he replied. "Mrs. Cooper told me. A remarkable fact. May God reward you."

"He has," said Anne, and smiled. She stood waving as he drove off with a great clatter. Then she turned her footsteps homeward.

Homeward! The word sent a thrill through her. This town, Brownes' Mill, was home, all the home she had ever known. Would it be so forever? Did Sam still want her?

All kinds of questions crowded into Anne's brain as she came in sight of the church. Her footsteps slowed, too, and she realized all at once that she was afraid. She put her box down on the church steps and sat near it for a few minutes, drinking in the blessed peace and stillness of the town. The same, she thought gratefully, it looks just the same.

Slowly she got up and walked across the common. A few children ran ahead of her, shouting. Others whipped tops. Anne averted her eyes from the Brownes' house, but in her heart she vowed to visit them soon.

"Poor old people," she said to them in her mind. "If I stay here, I shall take good care of you."

She walked the length of the common to the blacksmith shop. She tried the door, but it was bolted. She walked past it to Sam's house in the rear. Smoke rose from the chimney, indicating that someone was there. Quickly she opened the door.

Sam was sitting in a chair, staring at the fire. He turned at the sound of the door opening. A look of amazement and delight washed over his face. He got to his feet. He stared.

"Anne?" he said softly, tentatively. It was if he were trying out the name. "Anne?"

Anne closed the door, put down her box, and came forward. "Yes, Sam," she said. "I have come back."

Sam felt for something at the side of his chair and knocked down a stick. Anne felt her heart contract. "Are you ill, Sam?"

"No. Hurt. Had an accident."

"What kind of accident?" Anne asked.

"Crushed my foot in the forge," said Sam. "I'll be well soon. How are you?" he asked formally.

"I was a soldier," Anne answered. "I was wounded . . . and afterward very ill." Then, in a rush, she added, "Sam, I have come home." Her eyes were full of love for him.

He seemed to understand, but his voice was incredulous. "To me?" he asked.

Anne stared at him silently, nodding her head. Tears brimmed up in her eyes. Not now, she thought, I will not cry now.

Sam's face became effused with wonder and joy. The gentle, plain face changed before Anne's eyes into the handsomest, kindest face she had ever seen.

Without a word he held out his arms, and she walked into them. As he folded them around her, it was like a door closing, a door that would shut out the storms of the world and keep in love and peace and safeness.

He murmured words she could not hear clearly, then he tipped back her head and looked into her eyes. He spoke again. "Almost the last thing I said to you will be almost the first. Again, Anne," he asked, "will you marry me?"

"Yes," said Anne, and her voice quivered with happiness. "Yes," she said again, and nodded to emphasize the point. "Yes, Sam, I will marry you."

More Books from The Good and the Beautiful Library

Daniel and the Drum Rock
by Florence Parker Simister

Just David
by Eleanor H. Porter

Jade Dragons
by Florence Wightman Rowland

Redwood Pioneer
by Betty Stirling

goodandbeautiful.com